ADOPTED JANE

ADOPTED JANE

by *HELEN F. DARINGER*

ILLUSTRATED BY KATE SEREDY

NEW YORK

HARCOURT, BRACE & WORLD, INC.

ఌ. ఌ. ఌ. CONTENTS ఌ. ఌ. ఌ.

꙳ ꙳ ꙳ *ADOPTED JANE* ꙳ ꙳ ꙳

TWO INVITATIONS

MATRON JONES pushed open the door of the nursery where Miss Fink was getting the babies ready for bed. "Do you know where Jane Douglas is?" she queried brusquely.

The unexpected voice so startled Miss Fink that she almost upset the granite basin in which she was scrubbing little Peter's grimy, wriggling hands.

Hastily she righted the basin with one hand and tightened her grip on the slippery Peter with the other. "My, but you gave me a start, Matron!" she said. "Jane? She was here just a minute ago, buttoning the twins." She raised her voice. "Jane! Jane Douglas!" she called in a cracked soprano. "You're wanted."

At the far end of the room two small figures appeared in the doorway. Supported from behind by a pair of invisible hands, the clean-scrubbed twins toddled forward, stumbling over the skirts of their long nightgowns. Behind them came a girl, bent slightly forward to steady them. The girl's dark hair was cropped close like a boy's, but as she lifted her head it was her eyes and not her hair that one would notice first. They were clear gray eyes, flecked with hazel and fringed with black lashes.

"Yes'm, here I am," she answered. Then, noticing the matron, "Yes, ma'am, Matron Jones, did you want me?" She gave the twins a gentle push in the direction of their cribs. Had she done something wrong again, or did Matron only want her to dust her sitting room?

"Finish your task, Jane. Then I shall speak with you in my room." Matron's voice was noncommittal; it might mean anything.

"Yes, ma'am," Jane replied obediently. Matron Jones closed the door behind her and Jane turned to help insert a yawning Peter into his nightgown.

Miss Fink complained about Peter's dirty apron. He had got into the coalbin again. Matron ought to put a new lock on the coal shed. Jane murmured "yes'm" from time to time so Miss Fink would think she was paying attention. She could not think of anything bad she had done lately, and Matron did not look cross; but you couldn't be sure. She hoped Matron wanted her to go downtown on the streetcar. Errands were ever so much more fun than dusting. Anything might happen on an errand. You might see a runaway horse and buggy or there might be a funeral with a brass band. You might even find a nickel.

Jane had once found a nickel in front of Klohr's grocery. The storekeeper said it did not belong to him and why didn't she buy some candy? It took her a long time to choose, for she had never before had a nickel to spend for candy. She decided upon peppermint sticks. They were two for a penny and had red and white stripes like a barber's pole. When she got back to the orphanage she broke each stick in pieces so everybody could have one. She gave Matron and Miss Fink a whole stick between them.

Of course you couldn't expect to find a nickel every time. Probably Matron only wanted her to dust. Jane pulled the sheet up over Peter's relaxed little body and tweaked his nose to make him laugh. He was too sleepy to do more than yawn.

A few minutes later she presented herself at Matron's door. "Sit down, Jane," said Matron. "Help yourself to an apple."

"Thank you, ma'am." Jane breathed the words with a sigh of relief. Matron did not offer you an apple when she intended to give you a talking-to.

She sat up straight on the edge of the Morris chair and balanced the apple on her knee. Matron did not like you to eat apples in her room. She did not like to hear you chew.

"A letter came this afternoon," said Matron Jones. She

reached across the sewing table for her workbasket. Jane could see a pale gray envelope standing endwise among the spools of black and brown darning cotton. "It's from Mrs. Thurman. She's sister-in-law to Mrs. Bryce Blackwood who's Chairman of the Board. Mrs. Blackwood's been tryin' for years to interest her in the orphanage. The most she'll ever do is send twenty-five dollars at Christmas time, though Mrs. B. says she's got plenty of money and nobody to spend it on but herself. And we do need an infirmary so much!" Jane knew that Matron's reproving frown was intended for Mrs. Thurman and not for her.

"Well," she continued, "she wrote a letter." Something in her voice, or perhaps the intent look in her near-sighted blue eyes, made Jane begin to feel excited. Was it possible that the letter was about Jane herself? She didn't dare ask. Matron did not like you to ask questions. She called it interrupting.

"She says in the letter she'll take a child for a month. She wants a girl about eight years old." Jane's heart gave a dull thump. She was too old. The lady didn't want anybody as old as Jane. "She wants one that's quiet and well behaved. She says she'll give her the best of care. Of course we haven't an eight-year-old to send, now that Susie and Florence have already been placed for the summer."

"No'm." In spite of the disappointment of her own brief

hope, Jane sympathized with Matron. She could see that she was worried.

"I can't make up my mind what to do." Matron reread the letter to herself. She pursed her lips in thought. "Seems a mortal shame to let the chance slip."

Suddenly she laid a plump hand on Jane's knee. The apple bounced to the floor and went rolling under the sofa. Matron ignored it. Her face was solemn. "I'm almost of a mind to send you, Jane Douglas! You're older than she wants and you're not pretty (I can tell from the way she writes that she wants a pretty one—they all do), but you're small for your age and you're well behaved when you try." She paused, but Jane knew she had more to say. She was used to Matron's ways.

Matron nodded reflectively to herself. "Yes, some folks might say I was takin' unfair advantage to send somebody right into her own house to work on her for that infirmary. But it seems to me we're justified, Jane."

Jane stared at Matron. "You mean me?" she asked, incredulous of her own hearing. "I wouldn't know what to say. She mightn't like it," she added anxiously.

"Just do the best you can. That's all anybody can do. Better people than you have failed lots of times. Anyhow a visit will be a nice change." From Matron's tone Jane knew the matter was settled. You did not argue with Matron. She told

7

you what to do and you did it.

"Yes, ma'am. When do you want me to go?" Jane felt as if she were somebody else, a stranger. She seemed almost to be two persons. In one part of her was a heavy, sinking feeling, as if she had swallowed something bad and was going to be sick. In another part a flame of excitement was beginning to kindle. She could feel the flame mounting and mounting within her, like trumpets shining and singing in a circus parade.

Matron seemed not to have heard the question. She sat with puckered mouth and forehead. "I've got another letter." She rummaged among the papers in the drawer of the sewing table. "Here, this is it." She extracted a page from a long white envelope. "It does seem too bad—" her eyes were moving back and forth across the page as she spoke—"just too bad. Here's a lady writes from Cherry Valley for a girl about your age. Not to help with the work, mind you. No, she says they've plenty of hired help. She wants someone to keep her niece company when she comes to visit. She says you could play in the orchard and go wading and ride horseback. She's well recommended, Mrs. Scott is. Her preacher sent a letter and he says she's a fine woman. Her niece's name is Letitia."

Jane's heart almost stopped beating. Was it possible that she, Jane Douglas, who never before had been invited for a summer outing, now had two chances? She gripped the edge of the chair to hold herself still.

"It's too bad," Matron repeated. Her tone was brisk but kind. "Myself, I'd rather see you go to Cherry Valley. You'd have a better time and maybe you'd put a little fat on you. Seems like you get thinner and thinner. But there's the infirmary."

"Oh, Matron Jones!" The exclamation was scarcely audible.

"I sure am sorry." Matron's faded blue eyes met Jane's beseeching gray ones with troubled sympathy. "But Mrs. Thurman sets July for your month, and Mrs. Scott says July twentieth."

"Why couldn't I go both places?" The words rushed forth as if by their own volition. Jane seemed first to be aware of them as they hung, poised and daring, in the motionless air between her and Matron.

"Oh, couldn't you please write to Cherry Valley and ask if I mightn't come a little later? If Mrs. Scott's as nice as you say, she wouldn't mind. Oh, please, Matron! I've never in all my life had a chance to go on a visit. I'll work twice as hard when I come back and never lose my temper or any-thing—'less it boils over before I can help it," she added in honest, hasty parenthesis. "And I'll try my very hardest to make Mrs. Thurman understand how much better it'd be for the children if they could have an infirmary to be sick in.

Oh, Matron, *please!*"

Jane's unaccustomed boldness shocked Matron. She believed in bringing up children to be seen and not heard. Gradually, however, the shocked expression yielded to a thoughtful pursing of the lips. "I'll consider the matter." It would not do to encourage Jane to be forward in expressing her opinions. "Good night, Jane."

"Good night, ma'am." Jane retrieved the apple and closed the door carefully behind her. Even the youngest children knew better than to let a door bang.

The two persons inside her, the heavy, afraid one and the shining, singing one, had been joined by a third. The third self was bold, determined. "She's got to let me go to Cherry Valley," it kept repeating. "I'll make her let me. If she won't, I'll run off and go. I'll run off where they can't ever find me and bring me back," it maintained stubbornly.

Underneath her excitement, however, Jane was still aware of something like a heavy knot within her. What if Mrs. Thurman wouldn't take her because she was too old? What if Mrs. Thurman didn't like it because she tried to explain about the infirmary? What if Matron wouldn't ask Mrs. Scott to let her come later? And what—oh, most painful thought of all—what if it should turn out that she had to stay at the orphanage after all, in spite of the invitations? As she contemplated this dreadful possibility she struggled with a lump in her throat almost as big as a walnut. She swallowed it resolutely, two or three times, until her throat was clear again.

She was glad the little ones were in bed. She needed to be alone, to think. She crossed the cinder-covered playground to where an apple tree grew against the high board fence. By the time she was settled in the crotch of the wide branch that overlooked the fence and the road, she began to feel more like her ordinary self. She looked across the way to see if the "young couple," as she called them, were at home. Yes, there they were, walking arm in arm between the zinnia bed and the row of tomato plants. The yellow cottage with its neat white picket fence had been built a year ago, but it still looked brand new. You could see that they took good care of it.

And there, pushing his shaggy old head and shoulders close between the young couple, came Shep. Jane loved that dog. Sometimes he poked his nose through the bars of the orphanage gate and let her pet him. When she was grown up and went to live in a house of her own she'd have a dog just like him, shaggy brown and white. She hoped there would be a dog at Cherry Valley, one that would follow her everywhere as if it were her very own.

The twilight deepened. On the streetcar track an interurban car rumbled past on its way to St. Louis. Across the road, in the gathering dusk, fireflies began to shimmer and sparkle. A sleepy robin left a note half sung. Slowly Jane climbed down from her leafy perch. Her thoughts were still flickering with excitement and hope, and she was reluctant to go indoors. She must be careful not to tear her dress. The next time she snagged a skirt, Matron had warned, there would be an end to tree-sitting. She was getting too old to climb like a tomboy anyhow, Matron said; she ought to learn to sit on a chair and sew and be ladylike.

With every step that brought her nearer the big frame building Jane's hopes grew dimmer. There was something about the walls, from which the windows stared like rows of blank eyes, that discouraged hope. Jane entered by the side door. The front door was for visitors and Matron. The back one led into the kitchen, and Cook refused to have the young'uns traipsing in and out, getting under foot and tracking in dirt.

Jane made her way quietly upstairs. On the second floor she stopped at Miss Fink's room to report that she had locked the side door and was on her way to bed.

"Matron says you're going to Danbury to stay a month with Miz' Thurman. Won't that be nice!" Miss Fink sounded aggrieved rather than pleased. "I'm sure I don't know how I'm expected to look after eleven babies with nobody to help me. Sometimes I wonder why I stay on at this place. It's

nothing but work, work, work, an' no thanks neither. A body can wear herself to the bone and nobody t'appreciate the sackerfize."

Jane did not know what to say. She felt sorry for Miss Fink, with her scrawny neck and faded, wispy hair. Nobody in the orphanage worked harder than Miss Fink, it was true, and yet it was almost as if she were not there at all. She was so little and mousey, she retreated so quickly into corners, she spoke so seldom except to complain, that it was not surprising that nobody paid much attention to her.

"Yes'm," said Jane, "you do work awful hard, Miss Fink. You take awful good care of the babies."

Miss Fink sniffed, whether in pity for herself or pride it would have been difficult to discover. Jane stood a few moments longer in the doorway, wondering whether she ought to go or stay. "Good night," she said at last.

Jane slept on the floor above, in the part known as the girls' dormitory. It was a somewhat pretentious name for the attic-like room with twelve iron cots and four washstands of varnished pine. There were drawers in the washstands, one for each girl who slept there. Now that it was summer and some of the children had gone to visit relatives and others had been temporarily "placed" with families, Jane had the dormitory to herself. It was rather lonesome, but she liked it.

Sometimes when the moon shone in and whitened the

walls and floor, and shadows lay deep like pools of velvet, she planned surprises. One of her favorite surprises was to fill a poor family's coffeepot with five-dollar gold pieces. In the morning when the mother went to make coffee she'd find the money. Sometimes she used it to pay off the mortgage, sometimes she bought new clothes for the family, and sometimes she spent it for dozens of presents for the children. Jane liked to make-believe.

She made-believe she was the lady who played the pipe organ in the Methodist Church. She had heard the pipe organ only two or three times, because the orphanage children went to the Baptist Sunday School. It was nearer and they did not have to wear out so much good shoe leather walking all the way across town to the Methodist Church. Besides, Matron was a Baptist. When Jane pretended to be the lady organist she sang to her own accompaniment—very softly, of course, so Miss Fink would not hear.

Jane liked to sing. At school the music teacher said she had a nice soprano voice. But somehow when there was a program with pieces to recite and solos and duets to sing, the teacher never selected her. Jane was pretty sure it was on account of her clothes. She did not blame the teacher. All the other girls had nice dresses to wear on program days, and of course Miss Chapman did not want anybody in the kind of clothes the orphanage children wore standing on the platform in front of visitors. Still, it was hard to sit at your desk in the back row while Ruby Haines marched up to the rostrum to sing *My Heart's in the Highlands,* tossing her stubby braids and switching the accordion pleats of her red mohair skirt until the white ruffles showed on her petticoat. Ruby's voice squeaked when she sang the high notes, but her father was a member of the School Board. Jane's notes were always round and true. It was not vain to think so. It was the truth.

One reason she pretended things like surprises and playing the organ before she went to sleep was that she could not read. Occasionally she sneaked a book into the dormitory, but the odor of the kerosene lamp always betrayed her. Miss Fink would come tiptoeing upstairs to peer into the room. "I thought I smelled a lamp," she would announce as triumphantly as if she had cornered a burglar. She would pounce cat-like upon the lamp, turn down the wick, blow out the flame, and retreat downstairs. She never reported to Matron, however, that Jane was breaking the rules. Jane was grateful to Miss Fink for that.

Tonight there was no thought of books or make-believe. She longed for real things—a girl named Letitia for a friend, a brook to wade in, a horse to ride. Just to think of living like other girls in a real house with a family sent a shiver of delight down her back. Oh, she hoped Letitia and Mrs. Scott would like her! She'd try her very best to remember to be quiet and biddable. She'd always let Letitia have her own way. She'd offer to help Mrs. Scott with the housework, even though there was plenty of hired help to do it. And maybe when Mrs. Scott saw how useful she was, maybe, oh, maybe—

"There you go again," she admonished herself sternly. "Remember what Sammy Brown told you about your hopes getting too big for you, that time last summer when you thought Matron was going to send you on a visit? He told you you let yourself get all snagged up in hopes and then they give you a bad fall. Better not expect anything, and then you won't be disappointed. Sammy Brown's had experience with families. He knows what he's talking about." Although she couldn't really convince herself that it was a mistake to hope, she tried to tell herself that she would not be disappointed if the hopes did not come true. It was no use though. She knew she had never wanted anything so much in her whole life.

She leaned over the window sill and looked out. The moon was full, round and golden. Below, against the moon-whitened fence, the apple tree stood motionless, a tree half of silver and half of darkness. So silvery a stillness lay upon the world that she almost felt as if she could gather up the stillness in her arms and hold it.

2

THE JOURNEY

THE BABIES had been fed and were now napping. At least it was to be assumed that they were dutifully asleep since no sound floated down the stairs. Only three places were set at the long dining table. Matron Jones sat at one end, with Miss Fink on one side of her and Jane on the other. Until September brought the children back to the James Ballard Memorial Orphanage the room would remain as empty as a cornfield before the planting.

"Jane, you'll have to begin to learn table manners." Matron was dishing out the boiled cabbage and potatoes, a spoonful of each on Jane's plate. "If Mrs. Thurman's the kind of woman I think she is, she's probably finicky about manners. Don't you think so, Miss Fink?"

"Jane's manners are good enough for anybody when she tries," mumbled Miss Fink. She did not like boiled cabbage and Matron had put two big helpings of it on her plate. "Jane knows how to say *please* and *yes, ma'am* and *no, ma'am.* She knows not to reach across the table or eat with her knife."

"Yes, she's got good plain manners," admitted Matron, ignoring Miss Fink's sulkiness. "It takes fancy manners, though, to get along at a place like Mrs. Thurman's. Look, Jane." Matron balanced her fork daintily between forefinger and thumb, arching her little finger like the handle of a cup. "Hold your fork like this. Don't spread your hand out so wide and don't hold on so tight."

Jane shifted her fork to a position approximating Matron's. As soon as she tried to pick up a piece of potato, however, the fork slipped back to its accustomed angle.

"No, that's not right. Try again, Jane. Keep on trying until it comes natural."

She tried again, but with no better success. She thought to herself that if the potato were not hard as a rock she could manage better. Matron always picked out the soft potatoes for herself.

"Another thing," continued Matron. She was in an expansive mood. "Mrs. T. will probably have three or four knives and forks and spoons at every plate. One of 'em will be for soup, and one for pie and the others for ordinary things like meat and potatoes. Can you think of anything else they'd be for?" The question was aimed at Miss Fink.

Somewhat mollified by the indirect tribute to her social ex-perience, Miss Fink relaxed slightly. "There's coffee spoons, little ones they are, hardly bigger than dolls' spoons. Then there's ice-cream spoons. I ain't seen none myself, but my cousin was at a party where they had 'em. She says they're kind of half and half."

"Half and half what?" It struck Jane that anybody who could not eat ice cream out of an ordinary teaspoon was cer-tainly finicky.

Matron answered. It would not do to let Miss Fink feel too superior. "Half spoon and half fork, she means. And a very good way to describe them, too."

The lesson in table manners being concluded, Matron turned to more practical matters. "Remember not to talk to people on the train. Especially men," she warned. "They might kidnap you and then where would you be?" She did not wait for a reply. "I'll pin a dollar bill to your underskirt in case of emergency. Only in case of emergency, mind you! I'd pin your railroad ticket there too, but then how'd you be able to get it when the conductor came along? No, you just got to hold on tight to the ticket and not lose it."

"I was on a train once with a man that didn't have a ticket, and the conductor put him off," testified Miss Fink. "He said he'd lost it an' he didn't have any money to buy another one. I felt awful sorry for him, but the conductor put him off."

Matron nodded approvingly. "Let that be a lesson to you, Jane."

"Yes, ma'am." She would hold the ticket so tight that not even a team of wild elephants could get it away from her.

"Another thing. Keep to your seat. Don't go walking up and down the aisle. Well-behaved children don't traipse up and down in public places and call attention to themselves."

"No, ma'am—I mean, yes, ma'am."

"One more thing. Don't stick your arms or head or anything else out the window. People that stick their heads out the window often get them knocked off."

Up to this point Jane had followed Matron's admonitions with sober attentiveness. She was determined that no carelessness on her part, no ignorance of the rules of polite behavior, should blemish her visit. At Matron's warning about heads, however, she was seized with an almost irresistible desire to laugh. Her imagination conjured up the spectacle of people with several heads apiece, all stretching and craning to get the best view. She bit her tongue and pressed her right heel down hard on her left toes. Almost always she could keep from laughing if she pressed hard enough. She couldn't help speculating fleetingly whether, if a person had several heads that saw different things, he would see what the different heads saw all at the same time or one by one or just what he would see. "Yes, ma'am," she replied, a little stiffly because her tongue hurt where she had bitten it.

"Miss Fink will help you with the valise and put you in the care of the conductor."

Privately Jane determined to persuade Miss Fink, as soon as they were alone together on the way to the railroad station, not to say anything at all to the conductor. She was old enough to know where she was going. Besides, it was printed on the ticket and the conductor could read it for himself.

Matron spooned out the slippery whitish pudding, left over from the day before, which Cook brought in for dessert. As she handed Jane a portion, she considered whether or not it would be advisable to mention Cherry Valley. She had written to Mrs. Scott. She had been as persuasive as she knew how to be, for to do her justice, she had the children's welfare at heart. She felt that Jane deserved a change of luck.

Jane was only three when Matron Jones had come to take charge of the orphanage. Three is an age at which children have a fairly good chance for adoption. From the beginning, however, luck had been against Jane. She had scarlet fever, and then whooping cough. Even after she was well she looked frail and sickly. "Puny," Matron described her. If Jane had been a pretty child her opportunities would have been greater. The round-faced children with dimples were in demand, particularly if they had curls. Matron, who was a shrewd judge of character, sometimes felt tempted to warn the prospective foster parents that they were making a poor choice.

"Just because Lillie's got blue eyes and yellow curls is no sign she's good quality," she might have told them. "That thin little girl with the gray eyes is worth a dozen of Lillie." But she said nothing. She let the ladies make their own choices.

Perhaps something of all this had been in Matron's mind when she wrote to Mrs. Scott. She had tried to set Jane's case forth in as favorable a light as possible. But Matron was not a skilled letter writer. She found it easier to manage two or three dozen children than to write persuasive letters.

No, she thought, as she passed Miss Fink a second helping of pudding, she would not mention Cherry Valley. Probably nothing would come of her letter. Best let the child forget it.

Jane, for her part, kept trying to think of some way to bring the conversation around to Mrs. Scott. If only she knew whether Matron had written! If she had, then Jane might keep on hoping—though she had been too often disappointed to trust completely in hope.

Now Matron was giving Miss Fink some final advice about buying the ticket and what to tell the conductor. "Good-bye, Jane." She laid her plump, capable hand briefly on Jane's shoulder. "Have a nice time at Mrs. Thurman's and don't give anybody any trouble."

"Yes, ma'am. And I'll do the very best I can to persuade her about the infirmary."

"Don't ask her right out for it, child! That would never do. Surely you know better than to do that!" Matron was beginning to wonder whether she was not entrusting too weighty a responsibility to so inexperienced a courier.

"Oh, no, ma'am! I wouldn't think of asking her to give the orphanage money. Why, that would be just the same as begging." Jane's self-respect would no more permit her to ask for money than would Matron's. Decent people would rather go without than beg. It made no difference either to Jane or Matron that neither of them expected to profit from any gift Mrs. Thurman might make to the orphanage. "I'll let her know how things are when one of the babies gets bad sick, and she can let her conscience be her guide."

An hour later the train pulled slowly out of the station. Jane, flushed with excitement, waved good-bye to Miss Fink, who stood at the far end of the platform peering out from under her green cotton parasol at the red coaches and the puffing engine. Miss Fink nodded violently to show that she had at last located the window where Jane sat. She bobbed the green parasol convulsively up and down by way of farewell and clutched at her teetering hat. Then the coach had passed the platform, and the traveler was on her way.

It was not the first time she had ridden on a train. The preceding summer the Baptist Sunday School had held a picnic at Lithia Springs. The trip had been made in a special coach attached to the local train. The car had been crowded and the children sat three or four in a seat, but it had been a memorable occasion. Fifteen miles to the Springs and fifteen miles back—Jane had relived those happy miles more than once in memory.

Compared with today's journey, however, that had been a minor adventure. Today she would travel seventy-two miles, through towns and country she had never seen. There would be rivers to cross and stations to stop at and people to see, people walking on strange streets or riding along in carriages. Jane could have hugged herself for joy. Instead, she sat up very straight and tried to look as if she were quite used to riding on the railroad.

This was a much nicer coach than the one she had ridden in before, she noticed. Her seat was covered with dark green plush—a little stiff and bristly to touch, as she ran her fingers over it—and there was a brass spigot for drinking water at the end of the car. As soon as she saw the spigot she got thirsty, but Matron's injunction not to traipse up and down the aisle was still ringing in her ears.

There were not many people in the car, at least not at the front end where she could see. Across the aisle was a boy. She couldn't tell much about him because his back was toward her and his head was stuck out the window. He looked to be about Sammy Brown's age, or maybe older. Close beside him on the seat was a big market basket with a wicker cover. From time to time the boy reached backwards to feel whether the lid was tight, but he did not turn around. She wondered what he had in the basket. She'd study it a little later and see if she could make out.

In the seat in front of the boy a man was taking a nap, his face hidden under an outspread handkerchief. The pink-bordered square rose and fell with rhythmic regularity. Jane wondered how anybody could possibly go to sleep in so exciting a place as a railroad train. The man's coat was folded under his head for a pillow, and part of it dangled over the back of the seat. When the train lurched, the sleeve flapped lightly.

against the boy's basket. A pink carnation stuck out of the buttonhole in the dangling coat lapel. It looked almost too pink for a real carnation. Maybe it was a paper flower. Anyhow, it seemed funny for a man to wear a flower.

Jane longed to stand up in the aisle and look round behind her, but she kept a firm hand on herself. She must remember her manners. Perhaps a little later she would be able to think of some way to have a good look around without acting unladylike.

It was wonderful to have the scenery come rushing at you just outside your window. There were green fields of corn with teams plowing the long straight furrows; honey-colored fields of wheat and oats; and tall telegraph poles marching along beside you fast enough to keep step with the train. Now and then a little woods would spring up in front of your window as if by magic, and as quickly be whisked away again. The white farmhouses and the red barns, the cows knee-deep in willow-shaded pools or cropping the grass in green meadows looked like pictures in a library book.

The conductor's voice in her ear, calling "Tickets, all ticke-e-ts!" startled her. She had almost forgotten that she was on a train and that everything was real, not something she was reading in a book. She had a moment's panic lest she might have lost her ticket, but when she opened the little red pocketbook Miss Fink had given her, there it lay. The conductor punched it, stuck it in his pocket, and gave her a pink slip with two holes punched in it.

"Keep that, sister," he said. "It shows you've paid your way. You'll have to give it back before I can let you off the train."

She put the pink slip carefully inside the pocketbook beside the two nickels Miss Fink had given her. She was beginning to feel quite at home. She took off her round-crowned straw hat and laid it on the seat beside her. The elastic was too tight under her chin. She looked up to see whether her things were still safe in the baggage rack overhead. Yes, there sat the gray-blue canvas valise. Beside it lay her brown reefer coat. Miss Fink had advised against packing it. It would muss, she said.

Jane was rather sorry that the brakeman had not turned the valise so that the rope that tied it where the strap was broken did not show. The strap was of yellow leather and though it was stained it looked much better than the rope. The lady two seats in front had a new black suitcase. It looked very stylish in the rack. Matron had a suitcase too, a brown leather one, but she never used it because she never went anywhere.

The boy across the aisle was lifting the lid of the basket and peering inside. He was talking to something shut up there. A kitten perhaps, or maybe a puppy. Jane edged over toward the aisle. He looked like a friendly boy. Maybe if she sat where he could notice her he would say something. Then she could ask. She hoped it was a puppy he had. It might even be two puppies. The boy let the cover drop and turned again to the open window.

Jane kept her eyes on the basket. She just had to know what was inside, for something was certainly making it rock slightly, first to one side and then to the other. The lid began to rise, pushed upward from within. Suddenly there shot forth from under the cover a white-feathered rod. It was topped by a feathered flattish head with a broad yellow bill and two black eyes like shoe buttons. A duck! Who would ever have guessed it! A big white duck.

The duck blinked, stretched his long neck from side to side to make sure it was still in good working order, and opened his bill to a yawning V. Jane watched with fascinated gaze.

Something had fascinated the duck too, but it was not Jane. The black glassy eyes were fixed on the coat that swayed gently from the seat in front. Slowly, slowly, the long white neck was stretched, slowly the shoe-button eyes and bright yellow bill advanced toward the pink flower in the buttonhole. Jane watched as if hypnotized. Then with so unexpected and swift a movement that her eyes could scarcely follow, the broad yellow bill gaped open and snapped shut again. The pink carnation had vanished!

The boy must have felt the movement. He turned and quickly cupping the duck's head in both his hands, pushed it down into the basket. He fastened the cover securely in place. He did not even glance in Jane's direction. Almost immediately afterwards the man reached back for his coat. After he had pulled it on, he glanced around on the floor as if he had lost something. Jane knew what he was looking for, but she said not a word. Nobody in the whole world knew what had become of the pink carnation except herself— her and the duck. She almost laughed out loud.

At the next stop the man got off. So did the boy with the basket. Jane giggled. She couldn't help wondering whether it was a real flower the duck had swallowed. If it was paper it must have tickled his throat as it went down.

"Are you going far, little girl?" An old lady with a hooked nose had stopped beside Jane's seat and was leaning over her.

"Yes, ma'am," Jane answered politely. The old lady's eyes bored like the gimlet Sammy Brown used to make holes in a board.

"Where you goin'?" The old lady's eyes were on the shabby valise overhead. Jane felt that she could see right into it, and was turning the mended clothes inside-out for inspection.

"To Danbury, ma'am." Jane's voice was faint.

"Speak up, little girl. I don't like mumblers. What'd you say?"

"To Danbury, ma'am." The words sounded so loud in Jane's ears that she was afraid everybody on the train could hear.

"Danbury? That's not far. That's close. You told me you were goin' a long way! What made you tell something that's not true?" The sharp voice made Jane feel guilty without quite knowing why.

She did not know what to say. She could feel her face burning. Her throat was stiff and dry.

"What's your name, little girl?" the inquisitor persisted.

Jane remembered what Matron had said about not talking to strangers. She did not like the old lady anyhow. What right had she to be prying into Jane's affairs? She wasn't really a lady. Real ladies do not poke their noses into other people's business.

"I'd rather not say, ma'am," she replied in a low voice.

Although the words were faint, the stranger seemed to hear perfectly. "Well, I never!" she exclaimed loudly, drawing herself up. She struck her pocketbook against the arm of Jane's seat. "Such a bad-mannered little girl I never did see! Can't even answer a civil question!" She stalked down the aisle, looking indignantly to right and left.

Jane stared out the window. She held her eyes as wide open as she could to keep tears from coming. She felt that everybody in the whole car was whispering about her behind her back. She wished she were back in the orphanage. She wished nobody had ever invited her for a visit. She wished she were dead.

"Would you mind if I sat with you? My seat is on the sunny side and I find it rather warm."

Jane swallowed the lump in her throat and looked around. A tall man in a dark suit was standing beside her. He looked nice, but she could not see him clearly because there were still a few tears in her eyes.

"Yes, sir—no, sir—I mean it's all right if you sit here." She picked up her hat and moved over to make room for him.

He opened his newspaper and began to read. As the minutes slipped by and he continued to read, she began to study him. She started with his shoes. She could look at them without his noticing. They were polished as shiny as new ones, almost like patent leather. His suit was so dark that it looked almost black in the shadows. His hands did not look like a man's hands although they were big and browned. They were not calloused the way men's hands are. He had a narrow gold ring on the third finger of his left hand. There was no stone in it. She wished it had a diamond. She had always wanted to see a diamond close up.

She glanced up and her gray eyes met his blue ones. He was smiling a little, as if they both knew a good joke. She was not quite sure what the joke was, but she smiled back.

"It's a good day for a train trip," he said. "I'm sorry to be getting off at the next station."

"Oh, I wish you were going all the way." He could tell by

her voice that she really meant it. "I'm going to Danbury."

"Danbury? That's a fine town. You'll like it. Nice people in Danbury, too."

"Are there many children living there?" Ever since she had first known she was going there, she had wanted to ask someone that question.

He gave the matter a moment's serious consideration. "I couldn't say exactly, but such a friendly place as Danbury is certain to have boys and girls."

"That suits me," said Jane. She was beginning to feel as gay as a meadowlark. "I'm going to visit for a month."

The man looked his pleasure at her announcement. "I think we ought to celebrate an event like that," he said. "I'll try to get hold of the butcher boy."

Jane wondered how a butcher boy could help celebrate anything, and why there should be a meat market on the train at all, but she felt too happy to bother her head about it. A man in an old blue coat approached, holding in front of him a basket of bright-colored pop bottles and bananas and oranges.

"Here you are," said her new friend. "What will you have, young lady?" turning to Jane.

She opened her purse. "Would this buy an orange apiece?" she inquired, taking out the two nickels.

"This is my treat, remember." He shook his head at her in mock reproof. "Put your money away for a rainy day."

Jane was suddenly aware of how bright the sunlight lay in little patches on the green plush seats. "We'll have two oranges," he addressed the fruit man. "The two biggest ones."

Jane had never seen an orange as big as the one he laid in her lap. She took it up and smelled it several times, inhaling with the clean fragrance the exciting smell of train cinders and July dust.

"Was that the butcher boy?" she asked, watching him peddle his wares down the aisle. "I thought you meant a real butcher boy, one that works in a meat market." She laughed at the joke on herself. "I guess I've got a lot to learn."

"You're not alone in that." Her partner laughed comfortably. "My daughter tells me that she knows more about some things than I do. How to do a figure eight on roller skates, for instance."

While he peeled her orange with a pearl-handled penknife which he took from his trousers pocket, Jane studied him again. He looked different now that she knew he had a daughter. She noticed the scattered gray in his thick brown hair, and how the little wrinkles around his eyes made his face look friendly, and how clean his hands were. Surreptitiously she tried to rub the train dust off her hands on the back of her black stockings.

The train whistle blew for the next stop. He rose to go. "It's been a pleasure to talk with you," he said, holding his

hat in his hand as if she were a grown lady. "I know you'll
have a good time on your visit. And if you don't object, I'm
going to ask you to keep my orange. I have so many things
to carry that I can't take it."

"You could put it in your pocket," Jane suggested. "It
hasn't been peeled yet. Mine tastes wonderful. Try it."

He took a section of her outstretched orange, popped it into
his mouth, dropped his orange into her lap, smiled, waved his
hat, and was gone. Some of the brightness seemed to go out
of the car with him.

Jane stepped out into the aisle to look after him. Then she
got a drink at the water cooler and turned to look behind her
at the rest of the car. It was practically empty. People had
either got off at the back door, she supposed, or else they had
not got on the train at all.

She felt light and happy, even happier than when she first
began the journey. It was as if a weight had been lifted from
somewhere inside her. Everything was going to be all right.
Mrs. Thurman would not mind because Jane was too old and
her hair was straight. There would be girls and boys to play
with in Danbury. It was a fine town.

As she thought about it, she was almost certain it would
have a park with rope swings and an iron fountain and a white
wooden bandstand where a brass band played on Saturday
nights. Jane would walk through the park when she went on

errands for Mrs. Thurman. Every day she would dust Mrs. Thurman's furniture for her and help with the dishes and always keep her room tidy and not make extra trouble for anybody. She hoped Mrs. Thurman would take her to the park some Saturday night to hear the band play. She felt almost sure that Mrs. Thurman would, but if she didn't, it would be all right.

She was going to visit for a whole month. She was going to live in a house just like other people. Perhaps—but no, she put the thought aside as too daring. Still, things like that happened sometimes. They happened not only in books but in real life. In spite of her efforts to keep the hope from bobbing into plain sight, it forced its way into her mind where she had to think about it. Perhaps—perhaps Mrs. Thurman might adopt her. And then she'd never have to be an orphan in a Home again. Never.

"Danbury," the brakeman was shouting. "Danbury!"

Jane did not know how he knew that she was planning to get off at Danbury, since it was the conductor who had taken her ticket, but he reached up into the rack and brought down her valise and coat.

She handed him the pink slip with the two holes punched in it and asked him if he would please give it to the conductor. Almost before she realized what was happening, she was following him down the aisle and had descended the steps to the station platform.

The engine blew a shrill blast. A black puff of smoke and cinders billowed upward in the sunshine and then drifted down to settle on Jane's straw hat and limp, blue cotton dress. Her journey was at an end.

3

MRS. THURMAN

JANE brushed off the cinders that had settled on the faded brown coat which hung over her arm. She straightened her hat and took a firmer grip on the red pocketbook and the orange. Any minute now, Mrs. Thurman would be coming to meet her. Maybe she was waiting in the station and hadn't heard the train pull in. Jane would have gone inside to tell her she was already here, but it would not be safe to leave the valise on the platform.

Minute after long minute dragged by. Jane grew more and more uneasy. Perhaps she had made a mistake. Perhaps she had got off at the wrong place—but no, a big sign under the station eaves proclaimed this to be Danbury. Perhaps she had arrived on the wrong day. Maybe it was tomorrow she was expected.

Perhaps—perhaps when Mrs. Thurman got Matron's letter

she decided she did not want her. What could Jane do? The dollar pinned to her petticoat and the two nickels in her pocket-book would not buy a ticket back to the orphanage. It cost three cents a mile to ride on the train. Three times seventy-two was two hundred and sixteen. Where could she ever get enough money to make two dollars and sixteen cents? How could she ever explain to Matron and Miss Fink that she had had to come back because she was not wanted? The prospect left her forlorn. Her courage dwindled away.

She swallowed the lump in her throat and brushed away a few tears with the back of her hand. As she did so, the scent of the orange penetrated her despair. She took a deep sniff, and then another. The smell made her feel better.

Of course Mrs. Thurman would come to get her, she told herself sensibly. She wouldn't forget about meeting the train. She was just late. Jane was sometimes late herself. She felt a spring of confidence begin to well up. Things happened to delay you; you could not find one of your stockings, or some-one wanted you to help, or else you did not notice what time it was getting to be.

Jane seated herself on the valise and prepared to wait. The shadows under the row of box-elder trees were stretching longer and longer, but the sun was still hot. She folded the brown coat carefully and laid it across her knees with the pocketbook on top. She was glad the pocketbook was red and not black or brown. The orange she held in her hand. From time to time she took a deep sniff of it. Of course things would turn out all right, she tried to assure herself.

A carriage was coming down the shady street. The horse's hoofs stirred up little low clouds in the dust. A boy was driving, a boy who looked big enough to be in high school. She wondered where he was going all by himself. It seemed too bad not to take somebody out riding with you when you had a whole two-seated carriage.

The carriage stopped at the station. The boy wound the lines around the lower end of the buggy whip and stuck the whip back into the socket. He strolled leisurely towards the platform. Jane held her breath. She would not let herself believe that the boy was coming for her. Still, he might be. It didn't do any harm to hope. He disappeared inside the waiting room. A minute or two later he reappeared, his hands in his pockets, his cap pushed back off his forehead. He strolled toward Jane, keeping his eyes leveled at something just beyond and over her head, whistling nonchalantly as he came.

When he was directly in front of her, he stopped. "Are you going to Mrs. Thurman's?" he asked. He had brown eyes and his voice sounded a little husky. He cleared his throat.

"Why, yes, I am," replied Jane. It was difficult to keep her voice casual. She was so relieved that somebody knew about her and that she was not going to have to wait all night at the station that she could hardly make the words sound natural. "I'm waiting for Mrs. Thurman now. She'll be along almost any minute, I expect."

"She can't come. She's got company. She sent me to get you. These your things?" He pointed to the valise.

Jane nodded, wordless with relief.

"Here, you take the coat and pocketbook. I'll fetch the grip. Don't get into the buggy till I get there. The horse might scare and run away." He lifted the valise by the knotted rope handle.

Jane followed him, a step or two behind. He shoved the baggage into the back seat and waited for her to get in beside it. "Oh, please, would you mind if I rode in front?" she begged. "I've never ridden in the front seat, and this is such a beautiful carriage."

"Ride in front if you want to," he consented without enthusiasm. Then, after they were both seated and he had taken up the reins, "This isn't a carriage, you know. It's a surrey."

Jane did not know, but she was glad to be told. She wondered what the difference was, but it seemed wise to postpone the question until she knew him better. "My, but you're a good driver," she commented later. "The way you turned the corner and didn't run into the boy on the bicycle!"

"Aw, that wasn't anything." Although he spoke with affected indifference, Jane could see he was pleased that she had noticed. "In summer I always drive Mrs. Thurman's horse for her."

Jane wondered whether this was Mrs. Thurman's horse. She did not ask. Boys don't like to be asked questions, she knew. "Danbury looks like a big town," she said.

"Yes, it's quite a place," he granted. "It's the county seat. It's the biggest town within fifty miles." By this time they had turned another corner and were driving down a broad paved street. The houses on either side were large and new looking. "That white house with the screened-in porch is where our Congressman lives. Sometimes he's sitting on the porch, but not this afternoon. Out getting votes, I 'spect!" He laughed at his own little joke and Jane laughed with him.

"This is Prairie Avenue," he informed her after some minutes' silence. "All the big bugs live on this street."

"Does Mrs. Thurman live on Prairie Avenue?" If she was as rich as Matron said, of course she lived there, but still it kept the conversation going if you asked a question now and then to show you were interested.

"Nope." He shook his head. "She's got an old place. I think her family always lived there; or her husband's, I don't know which. Anyhow, it's not up-to-date like these on Prairie. It's all right though. She's got everything fixed comfortable. She's got a nice big yard and stable. Some of these new houses haven't got yards big enough to swing a cat in."

43

Then Mrs. Thurman did not have much money after all. She lived in an old house. Matron had counted on her having a lot of money. More than she knew what to do with, Matron had said. If Mrs. Thurman could not afford to build herself a new house on Prairie Avenue, Jane certainly did not believe she could afford to give money away—no matter how badly the orphanage needed an infirmary. Jane would have to explain to Matron how things were. Matron would be disappointed. And Miss Fink too. They both wanted that infirmary more than anything. Jane felt disappointed herself.

Now that her mind was awakened to noticing it, she observed that the carriage—or rather, the surrey—was not the least bit new. There were deep scratches in the dashboard. They had been painted over with black paint, but they still showed quite plainly. The leather cushions looked shabby too, and some of the buttons in the little hollows of the ridges were missing. No, she certainly could see for herself that Mrs. Thurman had no money to spare.

Jane was a little ashamed to realize that she felt relieved, yes, actually relieved because Mrs. Thurman was not rich. Now that she did not have to worry about it any longer, she had to confess to herself that all along she had been somewhat troubled. She had never carried on a conversation with a rich person. Of course she had spoken to Mr. Parker, who owned the biggest department store on Broadway. He was superin-

tendent of the Baptist Sunday School. He often stopped by
the pew where Jane's class met and asked how the Bible lesson
was going. That was not like carrying on a real conversation
though. All you had to say was, "Just fine, sir, thank you."
Yes, it was a load off her mind to learn that Mrs. Thurman
was just like anybody else.

The horse jogged on at a leisurely pace. The driver flicked
his whip now and then to shoo a fly away or to point out an
especially handsome house. Jane was glad he was not driving
fast. She wanted the ride to last as long as possible. "My
name's Jane," she said after a while, "Jane Douglas. I forgot
to tell you."

"I knew it already. Mrs. Thurman told me." He turned to
look at her. "I'm Richard Matthews. Almost everybody calls
me Richie. You can too if you want to."

"Oh, thank you." She felt so grateful that she wanted to
do something for him, something very nice. "Won't you take
this?" She laid the orange in his lap. "I just finished eating
one and I couldn't eat another." That was not strictly true,
but still it wasn't really a fib either, the way she meant it.

"Thanks." He accepted it carelessly. She knew by the way
he looked at the orange, however, that he was glad to have it.
They turned a corner. "I've got a sister about your age." He
glanced at her again. "She's bigger than you. Her name's
Cecilia. Everybody calls her Cissie."

"Cecilia's a lovely name." Jane sighed a little, thinking of her own plain name. "And Cissie's a good nickname," she hastened to add. "Do you live next door to Mrs. Thurman?" She knew him well enough now to begin asking questions.

"Nope, about a block away. We live on the street back of her. You don't have to go all the way 'round, though; you can cut across lots."

Jane drew a deep breath. Already in imagination she was cutting across lots to Cissie's house and she and Cissie were planning good times together.

"Watch old Polly now," said Richie. He put the whip back into the socket and let the lines fall slack. "She knows the way home, you bet. Just watch her edge over. She knows she ought to keep to the right, but she always begins to pull over when we get nearly there. See how she picks up her gait, too." It was true; Polly was trotting. "Now watch her turn into the driveway—how careful she is to swing out far enough not to bump the back wheels against the coping."

Jane made only a pretense of watching. It was really too much to expect her to give the horse her undivided attention. She had to look at the house where she was coming to visit. It was a brick house, painted dark gray, and shaded by tall oak and maple trees. Anybody could see that it was not a new house, it was so plain and old-fashioned.

She caught sight of a fountain on the sloping green lawn,

a round sunken basin with two little children almost life-size, made of iron, holding an iron umbrella over their heads. The little girl was holding up the edge of her iron dress to keep it dry and one of the legs of the boy's pants was rolled above his knee. There was no water falling on the umbrella and the cement basin was quite dry. Jane hoped with a quick, insistent hope that some sunny afternoon Mrs. Thurman would let her turn the water on. She could imagine it splashing like real rain against the umbrella and spilling over to wet the iron children. She had never dreamed that Mrs. Thurman would have a fountain in her front yard.

Richie stopped at the side entrance. "Well, here we are," he announced. "I'll get your things out of the back seat." He dropped the valise with a plop in front of her and shoved her coat into her arms. "Go on in," he instructed her. "They're expecting you." He led Polly toward the stable.

Jane heard the pebbles in the driveway grind and scrape as the wheels passed over them. For some reason the grinding and scraping made an echo inside her, as if she were hollow. "Don't be silly," she reprimanded herself sternly. "Of course she wants you. Didn't she write a letter?"

The door opened and a woman appeared on the porch. She was a large woman with gray hair pulled back tight from her flushed face. The sleeves of her blue calico dress were rolled neatly above her elbows, and her large white apron was snowy.

"Howdy'do, Jane! Come right in. We've been lookin' for you this past half hour now. Richie must have stopped somewhere on the way." Her voice sounded hearty. Jane liked her immediately.

"Didn't I tell you!" Jane whispered triumphantly to herself, only not so anybody could hear, of course. "Old fraidy cat, thought Mrs. Thurman didn't want me!" She was positively scornful of her inside self.

"No, don't you heft that grip. It's too heavy." The warm cheerful voice gave Jane no time to say a word. "Here, let me have it. It won't be nothing for me to lift." She bent over and picked up the valise. "Why, it's not heavy at all," she exclaimed in surprise. "It's so big I thought it must weigh a ton."

"Yes, ma'am." Jane took advantage of the momentary pause. "The grip's bigger than I needed. It was the only one left."

She followed the valise across the screened porch and into a cool, darkened room. "Come right on upstairs," the voice invited. "We'll get you settled so you can wash and clean up a little. I've got supper on the stove and have to get back in a hurry." She apologized for her haste.

They ascended a walled-in flight of stairs and came out into an airy hall, into which several doors opened. "Sorry to take you up the back stairs on your first visit, but it's much the quickest," her guide explained. "Now, here's your room."

She set the valise down inside a sunny, pink-flowered room. "You'll find towels and soap in there," pointing to an inner door. "There won't be time for a bath, but you can wash up. Soon as you're ready, come downstairs. You'll find me in the kitchen."

"Thank you, ma'am. I'll be quick as I can." Jane doubted whether she had been heard, for already the stairs were creaking under the impact of heavily descending steps.

She stood still and looked about her, drawing a deep breath of delight. What a pretty room! It was much prettier than the rooms in Miss Fink's *Ladies' Home Magazine*. Pale pink morning-glories with leaves of pointed green made patterns on the white wallpaper. The furniture was pale yellow. It must be bird's-eye maple, she thought, it was so smooth and as shiny as satin. The wood had little curlicues in it like the curlicues in watered silk. Yes, it was just like the bird's-eye maple described in *The Girl of the Limberlost*. There was a dressing table with a white embroidered doily on top and a long oval mirror. In front of the dressing table was a little bench. There were a rocking chair and a low set of glassed-in bookcases, all of the same smooth, satiny wood. She must see what the books were—she hoped they weren't ones she had already read. Goodness gracious, she was dawdling! She mustn't make Mrs. Thurman wait supper for her! On the very first day, too!

She tugged at the straps of the valise and struggled with

the knotted rope. In a place where everything was so shining clean, she'd have to put on a clean dress for supper. She had been careful of the one she had on, but it had got wrinkled and dusty in spite of her care. At the Home you wore a dress until it was really dirty, but she guessed maybe you didn't at Mrs. Thurman's. She could iron her own dresses if somebody else would wash them. Maybe she could even wash them if Mrs. Thurman had too much to do.

At last the stubborn knot yielded. She took out the dresses, all four of them, and laid them on the bed. There was the one she had torn on the apple tree, with a big patch of darker blue right in front where it showed. That wouldn't do. She must look her best. The next one was worn thin, but Matron thought she could still get some wear out of it if she remembered not to stretch and pull when she had it on. The other two dresses had been new last fall, a brown checked seersucker for school and a blue gingham for Sunday School. Did she dare? Yes, she would put on her best Sunday dress.

When she opened the washroom door she was astonished to see that it was not a washroom at all, but a real bathroom, with a white tub that stood on four white claws and looked as if it were made of thick china. They had bathtubs at the orphanage, for the building had been done over the year before and modern plumbing and gas fixtures installed. The tubs were not like this though. They were made of galvanized zinc and had a wooden ledge around the top. She wished Miss Fink could see this house. Miss Fink liked nice things. She'd take pains to describe it to her when she got back to the Home.

Jane scrubbed her face so vigorously that soap got into her eyes. Better get soap in her eyes, she thought, than not get clean and then rub off black on the clean towels. She had never seen such white towels. And they had been ironed until there was not a wrinkle in them. The soap had a faint smell of something sweet, she couldn't think what. The bar felt smooth and soft; it reminded her of a big rounded spoonful of vanilla ice cream. As she ran her old black comb through her short dark hair, she laughed to herself at the idea of washing in ice cream.

She polished the dust off the toes of her shoes with a piece of paper. If it were not her first visit at Mrs. Thurman's, she would change into her old shoes. These were still so stiff that they rubbed blisters on her heels.

She took a hasty look at herself in the mirror above the dressing table to make certain that her hair was parted straight. Her eyes looked out at her from the mirror, shining with excitement. "Isn't it wonderful?" she whispered to the face in the glass. "Exactly like a story in a book!" She was still fastening the last button as she hurried down the stairs.

The kitchen was empty, but the cooking pans on the gas range were evidence that Mrs. Thurman was not far distant.

Jane seated herself on a tall stool beside the kitchen table. She would have liked to help with the supper, but it might seem meddlesome.

The door swung open to admit an elderly man carrying a small milk pail. "Well, well," he said. His sharp little eyes surveyed Jane from head to foot. He straightened his bent shoulders. "So you got here, did you?"

"Yes, sir." Jane could not be sure whether he was cross or only surprised to see her. "I came on the train this afternoon."

He seemed not to hear. "Tell Aggie the cream ain't so thick. Pasture's dryin' up, this long hot spell." He set the cream inside the icebox, rattling pans and dishes as he did so.

Again the door swung open, this time to admit Jane's new friend. Indeed she seemed by now an old friend. She nodded cheerfully at Jane, but addressed herself to the man who was just closing the icebox. "Fetch the cream?"

"Oh, it's you, Aggie? Didn't hear you come in. Yep, I brought it, but it ain't what it ought to be, what with this danged dry weather."

"Sh—we'll have no swearing, Abner. Remember there's somebody else in the room." She gave a significant nod in Jane's direction.

"Pshaw, Aggie, don't be so pernickety. *Danged* ain't swearin'. It wouldn't hurt a baby to hear it, much less a big

girl like her. It don't upset you none if I say danged, does it?"
He winked elaborately at Jane, who could only giggle in
reply. "There now, Aggie, you kin see for yourself she's not
hurt. Where in tarnation did I lay my cap?" He looked around
on table and sink and chairs.

Jane laughed out loud. She couldn't help it. She felt so
happy and the supper smelled so good and it was so funny to
see him hunt his cap while all the time it was right on his
head. She pointed to the top of her own head. He put up his
hand and, feeling the cap, grinned sheepishly. "Pshaw!" He
repeated the word to himself, "Pshaw!"

Jane scarcely noticed when he sidled out the back door, for
the oven door had just been opened and a delectable odor
flooded the room. It was chicken, roasting in the oven, big
plump pieces, sizzling hot, golden brown. "My, that smells
good," she said, watching the oblong baking pan as it was
lifted out of the oven and set down over an unlighted burner
at the back of the stove. "I could almost eat the smell, it's
so good."

"I'm pleased to hear it. Mebbe you wouldn't mind obligin'
me by trying a piece to make sure it's cooked through. Careful—don't burn yourself. It'll cool off in a minute an' then
you can take it in your fingers."

Jane could hardly wait for the drumstick to cool off; in fact
she blew on it surreptitiously to hasten the cooling. The

chicken tasted even better than it smelled. The outside was just crisp enough to be crunchy and the inside was so tender that it almost melted when she bit into it. As she ate, she watched the pieces being lifted off on a white and gold platter. She thought she could eat every single piece all by herself without stopping.

"Soon as I make the gravy and season the peas, I'll mash the potatoes. I always do them last because mashed potatoes don't improve with standin'. They get soggy. Now," wiping her hands on a clean towel and passing it to Jane, "now I'll go in and see if the preacher's gone. I think I heard the front door a while back."

Jane was somewhat puzzled. Did the preacher live here, and if he did, why would he leave just at suppertime? If he smelled the chicken and gravy and saw the big lump of butter melting on top of the peas, and the little white and gold bowl of strawberry preserves that had just been poured out of a glass Mason jar, she was sure he would have stayed. She had never been so hungry in her life. The drumstick had only whetted her appetite.

"There now, I guess everything's ready 'cept the potatoes. Are your hands clean? Come on then, Jane, into the room. Mrs. Thurman will be expecting you."

"Did you say Mrs. Thurman?" Jane thought her ears must be playing a trick on her.

"Sure I said Mrs. Thurman. Who else did you think I'd say?"

"Why—oh—I thought you were Mrs. Thurman. Isn't this your house?"

"Land sakes no, child. I'm Aggie—Aggie Simpson. I've worked for her since before we was both married and she was Cora James and lived here with her pa and ma. What ever made you think I was her?" Aggie's face turned a little redder with pride. She couldn't help being flattered that the child had mistaken her for Cora Thurman. She was a smart little girl too, anyone could see that.

Taking Jane by the hand as if she were a small child, she conducted her through the hall into a room beyond the dining room. A lady in a deep chair was looking out the window. "Here's Jane Douglas, ma'am," Aggie announced, letting go of Jane's hand and projecting her forward with a kindly thrust. Jane longed to regain the security of Aggie's hand, but she was already out of sight.

The lady looked at Jane. "So you are Jane," she said, holding out her hand. "I was expecting a larger girl. Mrs. Jones' letter led me to expect an older child."

Jane advanced and shook the proffered hand politely. "Yes, ma'am. I'm not very big for my age."

"I see." Mrs. Thurman motioned her to be seated. Jane sat stiffly on the edge of a straight chair. "Did you have a

55

pleasant journey?" Mrs. Thurman's voice was quiet, not hearty like Aggie's.

"Yes, ma'am, I had a pleasant journey."

"Did Richard meet you?"

"Yes, ma'am, he met me."

Neither could think of anything else to say. They sat facing each other while each covertly studied the other and tried to give the impression of being at ease. Jane saw a woman with faded brown hair curled in soft bangs and knotted high on her head. Her face was not exactly pretty, but it almost was, Jane decided. Her eyes were blue and she had a fair complexion. She looked as if she was not very happy. Or maybe she was tired. She didn't look complaining though, like Miss Fink. It was easy to see that Mrs. Thurman was a lady. A real lady, not the kind who had scolded her on the train. Jane's spirits sank a little lower at the memory.

What could she ever talk about to Mrs. Thurman? Ordinary ladies, like Miss Fink and Aggie and the Sunday School teacher, talked to you about ordinary things, such as what you studied in school and whether the weather was hot enough for you and what would you like to be when you grow up? Mrs. Thurman would not be interested in any of those things.

Nor would a lady like Mrs. Thurman be interested in hearing about things that happened at the orphanage, about how Jimmy had broken his arm and Katie had broken a window

and the time Cook lost her temper and threw a pan out the kitchen window and Matron sailed right into the kitchen and gave her a good piece of her mind and Cook said she wouldn't stay another day to be talked to like that. But she did stay and she was still there. Still cooking boiled potatoes and boiled cabbage and bread pudding and stewed apples and prunes. Something like homesickness swept over Jane. If only she were in the orphanage right now, watching Cook put the dried apples to soak!

Aggie spoke from the doorway. "Supper is served, ma'am."

Homesick though she was, Jane noticed that Aggie had rolled down her sleeves and that there emanated from her a faint, delicious odor of fried chicken and gravy.

"Come, Jane." Mrs. Thurman rose. "Shall we have supper?"

4

NEW DRESSES

Supper did not go well. Topics for conversation eluded Jane. Just in time she caught herself on the point of commenting, "What a big tablecloth!" and "That's a lot of chicken for two people." It was not good manners to make remarks about other people's belongings. It was not polite, and it might hurt their feelings. By the time she'd think of a mannerly remark it was either too late or else it wasn't the kind that would interest a lady like Mrs. Thurman.

The supper itself offered a number of obstacles. Mrs. Thurman served Jane's plate and Aggie placed it in front of her, though Jane sat so close she could easily have reached it herself and saved Aggie the trouble. She wished Aggie would sit down with them. She supposed she'd rather eat in the kitchen with Abner. Jane did not blame her. The kitchen was more comfortable, and it wouldn't matter if you spilled something.

Aggie was not so friendly as she had been. She hardly spoke except in a distant kind of way. Jane felt almost glad when Aggie departed. Now there was only one person to watch how she ate, instead of two. At the orphanage, on the rare occasions when chicken was served, Matron let the children take the pieces in their fingers because it is so hard to hold a piece on your plate with a fork while you cut it with a knife. Of course Jane couldn't use her fingers at Mrs. Thurman's. It would not be good manners. She sawed awkwardly at the wishbone, which slipped and slid and skidded and finally bounced almost off the edge of her plate.

The peas that had looked so meltingly green under the golden butter were as slippery as the chicken. Then she observed that Mrs. Thurman was using for her butter a little knife with which Jane had not known what to do. It lay on a small plate near her big one. Now she realized that not only should she have used the little knife, but she should have laid her bread on the little plate. She was too embarrassed to eat the slice which she had so carefully buttered and spread with strawberry preserves. Only the mashed potatoes proved satisfactory. They were very good indeed—smooth and fluffy and flecked with specks of black pepper and tasting of butter and cream.

"Eat your chicken and peas, and let me give you more,

Jane," Mrs. Thurman urged. "No wonder you're thin!"

If only she had offered her more mashed potatoes! Jane watched hungrily while Aggie carried out the plates, one at a time, and then the platter of chicken, the peas, the mashed potatoes, the strawberry preserves, and the cubes of pale green watermelon pickle. Her spirits revived with the dessert, however. It was ice cream, a heaped mound in her gold-edged sauce dish, tasting luxuriously of vanilla. When she thought about it afterwards in bed, she realized that there were no ice-cream spoons. Just ordinary teaspoons. They were old, with thin handles, though they had been shined to look like new.

There were other indications that Mrs. Thurman was not wealthy. As they sat in the back parlor after supper, Mrs. Thurman with her knitting and Jane balanced uncomfortably on the edge of a chair, she had plenty of time to study the room. None of the furniture was new, not even the books that lined the shelves on two sides. She hoped some of the books were for girls. She liked to read almost more than she liked to play. She noted a number of small tables—three, she counted. One would be enough to keep your sewing basket on and write letters and put a vase on. They looked very old-fashioned, but she supposed they were too good to throw away. The golden-oak table in the orphanage parlor was much newer.

"Have you ever been in Danbury before?" Mrs. Thurman

was asking.

"No, ma'am," Jane replied politely.

Another silence. In vain Jane sorted out her ideas to find a suitable remark.

"Do you knit, Jane?"

"No, ma'am."

There was a muffled scratching at the door and a tan and white collie pushed his way into the room. He walked sedately toward Jane, who sat without stirring while he sniffed gravely at her feet and knees. He turned around twice in a circle and lay down comfortably in the center of the rug. "Oh, please, do you think he'd let me pat him?"

Mrs. Thurman glanced up from her knitting in surprise. Could this lively, eager voice be the same that for the past hour had been tiresomely repeating *yes, ma'am* and *no, ma'am?* "Certainly. Rover enjoys attention."

Jane remembered to be ladylike. She bestowed two or three gentle pats upon Rover and reseated herself. Aggie interrupted the silence to summon Mrs. Thurman. Jane heard them going upstairs. When she was certain they were out of sight, she slipped quickly off the chair to crouch beside Rover. She stroked his tawny silken ears and smoothed his thick tan-colored coat and scratched him gently on the white spot under the chin. He thumped his tail to show his appreciation and yawned prodigiously.

Jane hugged him. "We're friends," she told him. "A girl's best friend is her dog."

When she went upstairs she found that someone had turned down the bed and hung her dresses in the closet. She meant to stay awake to think over all that had happened since she left Miss Fink at the railroad station waving the green parasol. Was it only today that she had been eating cabbage and boiled potatoes at the orphanage? It seemed ages and ages ago, so much had happened since then. But she was so sleepy that she had time only to think about the ice cream and the thin-handled spoons.

She would have liked to help with the work the next morning to show her good intentions, but Aggie sent her outdoors to play. Rover was nowhere visible. He might be in the stable, she thought, but she hesitated to step inside. It would be almost the same as going into a house where she hadn't been invited. If she had somebody to play with, it would be a good yard for hide-and-seek, there were so many big trees and bushes. She looked through the opening in the bridal wreath hedge. Why, it was country on the other side—a grassy field with cows and a horse.

Skirting the field was a road. It lay sunny and still in the morning air, as if waiting. Jane's heart leaped. She was free, she was visiting, she didn't have to stay in the yard. She could go on that road if she wanted to.

She walked quickly, not because she must return soon, but because something within kept urging her on. The road was empty. It was all hers—the tall Queen Anne's lace and sharp-petaled black-eyed Susans that lifted their heads above the wild grasses; the shag-bark hickory, ruffling its branches in the light breeze; the crow that cawed a noisy greeting from a cornfield.

Ahead of her was a clump of willows, bent aslant, and there the road curved. Adventure waited beyond the curve, she knew by the way her heart beat. She quickened her steps until she was almost running.

As she rounded the willow clump she saw something that brought her to an abrupt halt. Under the low-hanging branches sat a baby, all alone. He must have been nearly three years old, for he was the size of little Peter, but there the resemblance ended. This baby was brown as the hull of a ripe walnut, his black hair hung straight, his black eyes fixed her with a stare half defiant, half frightened.

Jane stood still. She knew that a baby has to have time to get used to strangers. She smiled at him and hummed the little coaxing tune that Peter liked, but he did not smile back. Jane could see that he had been crying. He wore a little tassel of smudged silk, a jumble of bright colors, and a string of green glass beads around his neck. Gradually Jane edged close. He was dirty; he couldn't have had a bath for a long time

Miss Fink would have insisted on scrubbing him at once, but Jane loved him just the way he was.

She plucked a long willow leaf and tickled him on the nose. He only blinked. She tickled him again. He put out his hand for the leaf and she let him have it. He wasn't so scared of her now. He made her think of the brown baby rabbit Sammy Brown had caught in the vegetable garden. She tried to entice him with a game of peekaboo, but though he watched her intently he did not change expression.

Jane persisted. At last, with the alluring rigmarole of *pat-a-cake, pat-a-cake, baker's man,* she won his confidence. He let her fold and unfold his warm-fingered fists to show him how to play, and when the game was learned he was almost quicker at it than she. He made no attempt, however, to say the words. Jane wondered if he didn't know how to talk.

Suddenly he gave a shrill cry and jumped to his feet. A woman was standing under the willow. How long she had been there Jane did not know. She only knew that she was a gypsy and so beautiful to look at that Jane gazed and gazed as if she could never have her fill of looking.

She was walnut brown like the baby and her hair hung in two long braids from under a scarlet 'kerchief knotted around her head. She had great moon-shaped gold earrings, and the front of her soiled yellow blouse was almost covered with long ribbons of bright fluttering silk, silver and gold and

66

green and blue and red. Her long skirts billowed out like a balloon—red and orange and bright green and purple—and the voluminous apron that topped them, bordered with torn embroidery, was as gaily flowered as wallpaper. It was her face though that held Jane's heart under a spell—the smooth brown cheeks and red, red lips and the dark eyes in level, fathomless gaze under the straight black brows.

The baby clutched at her to burrow his head under her wide skirts. There was a muffled squawk, an agitated flapping, and to Jane's intense surprise a fat white hen fell from under the bright-flowered apron. Calmly the woman set a bare foot upon the flopping fowl to hold it quiet. She addressed the child sharply in some strange language, and he emerged again into the open.

"Will the young lady have her fortune told?" The voice was wheedling, smooth.

Jane's heart contracted with longing. "No, thank you, ma'am. I haven't any money." She knew that you must cross a gypsy's palm with silver.

The princess (Jane was becoming more and more convinced that she was a gypsy princess) took Jane's hand in hers. "I tell the little lady's fortune for nothing—free." Her brown hand, as it brushed across first one, then the other of Jane's palms, felt like a wing—a brown thrush wing, Jane thought.

She scrutinized both of Jane's palms closely. She turned the hands over and back again, flexed the fingers. "Very good fortune," she said. "Lucky star. The little lady was born with a star of luck." She pointed to a tiny cluster of raying lines at the base of the forefinger.

Jane's heart pounded with delight; not so much because of the lucky star, although that made her happy too, but because she had had her fortune told. Told by a real gypsy. "Oh, thank you, ma'am!" She put her whole happiness into the words. "Thank you ever and ever so much!"

The gypsy gathered up the submissive hen and thrust it under the folds of her apron, swung the little boy on her hip, and strode off on noiseless feet. Jane stood in the shade of the trees watching. The bright figure seemed to glide rather than walk, swaying lightly as a willow in the sunny morning breeze.

Jane set her face toward Mrs. Thurman's again. Adventure had beckoned and she had followed the call. Now it was time to be her plain self again. An adventure couldn't last forever. "But I'll always remember it," she thought, hugging herself, "forever and ever."

Nobody was in sight when she reached the house. She looked aimlessly along the bookshelves to find a good book. Most of them had no conversation. They looked very uninteresting, practically all of them, except one with a blue and gilt cover entitled *The Wide, Wide World*. The front page had *Cora* written on it, and underneath, *From her loving Mother*. At first Jane supposed it was a geography book, but it wasn't. It was a story about a girl.

She was so absorbed in the story that it required a moment to come to herself when Mrs. Thurman said Cecilia Matthews had come to call. Jane would have liked to finish the chapter to know whether the stern aunt dyed the white stockings ugly gray (though she could hardly believe that even a long time ago a girl would really wish to wear white stockings); but of course it would not be polite to go on reading. Besides, she was glad to make Cecilia's acquaintance.

They sat in the back parlor, the three of them, Mrs. Thurman with a pillowcase to mend, Jane with her book wedged between her back and the chair, and Cissie. The latter was elegant in shiny rubber boots and a mackintosh lined with red plaid. She explained somewhat self-consciously that she thought it might rain, but Jane suspected the real reason was that the mackintosh and red-topped boots were new.

Cissie said, not looking in Jane's direction, that her mother thought it would be nice if she called on the new girl. Mrs. Thurman said that was very kind of Cissie and her mother.

Cissie said that Richie had gone fishing and, oh, yes, he had told her to ask if Mrs. Thurman would need him tomorrow. Mrs. Thurman said yes, she and Jane would be going to town.

Jane could not think of anything to say.

Cissie said there was a new family in the house next door to them. Mrs. Thurman said she knew it to her sorrow. Though she could not afford it she would buy the place rather than have a goat and chickens on a lot adjoining her property.

Still Jane could not think of anything to say. Cissie and Mrs. Thurman seemed to know each other so well that there was no place for her in the conversation. At last, with a kind of now-or-never feeling, she asked, "Have you a dog, Cissie?"

Surprised, Cissie turned on her chair and faced Jane. "No," she answered slowly, as if she were making up her mind about

Jane. "We had one, but it died."

"You must have felt awfully sad."

Again Cissie surveyed her. "No, I didn't. It was Richie's dog."

How could Cissie not have cared? "Why, a dog is just like a real person. If anything happened to Rover I'd feel dreadful. He's my best friend, almost." Oh, dear! She had not intended to speak out like that. It sounded as if she were scolding Cissie. She had not meant to. It was only that she couldn't bear to have people talk as if dogs did not have feelings the same as people.

Jane relapsed into uncomfortable silence. Cissie said she must go now. Mrs. Thurman invited her to stay for supper, but Cissie said no, thank you, her mother was expecting her.

Jane accompanied her to the edge of the lawn. Cissie said she must come over to see her some day and Jane said yes, thank you. Cissie did not sound as if she really meant it. The more Jane thought about it, the more she felt she did not blame Cissie. "You acted just like a dumbbell." Jane did not mince matters when she scolded herself. "No wonder Cissie thinks you're a stick-in-the-mud!"

She went upstairs early, taking the book with her. She didn't think Mrs. Thurman noticed. She could probably read in bed without Mrs. Thurman's ever knowing. Nevertheless, she would not do it. Mrs. Thurman might think it was sneaky.

She read while she got ready for bed, however, unlacing first one high shoe and then the other, unfastening the row of buttons down the back of her dress, unbuttoning her petticoat—lifting her eyes only when she turned a page.

The next morning Richie drove downtown. Jane sat with Mrs. Thurman in the back seat, careful not to wrinkle the blue gingham which Aggie had just washed and ironed though Jane had worn it only once. She wished Richie would say something to her, but he acted as if he hardly remembered her. If only she could think of something to talk about! Richie left them on Main Street and drove on to get a dozen glass Mason jars and a box of Van Houten's cocoa, to save Mrs. Thurman the trouble.

Jane could not help feeling excited as she entered the department store with Mrs. Thurman. The lady clerks stood behind the counters with their backs to the shelves of bright calicoes and ginghams and watched them as they went by. Jane sniffed the faintly musty, clean, dry goods store smell. She felt almost grown up, walking down the aisle. In front of the silk counter, where the edges of the flat bolts showed like bands of narrow ribbon—magenta, plum color, ashes of roses, dove gray—the gentleman clerk bowed. "Is there anything I can show you today, ma'am? We've just received a new shipment of fine French silks. A handsome length of salmon-pink satin, ma'am, and some fine reseda green."

Mrs. Thurman said thank you, not today. You could tell by the way she walked, with her head held up and not in any hurry at all, that she was a real lady. Jane noticed with pleasure the hushed whispering sound of her gray voile skirt against the gray taffeta petticoat.

In the rear of the store, where the stairway started up, a young lady customer sat on a stool. From a little wooden can with a curved spout like a sprinkling can the clerk was shaking powder into a pair of white kid gloves. Jane had never seen such long gloves. They must reach past your elbow. A young man in a light suit leaned close to the young lady. Jane would have liked to lean close to watch too, the young lady was so smiling and stylish and beautiful. Maybe they were Engaged. As she followed Mrs. Thurman up the stairs she kept looking back. She couldn't remember seeing an engaged couple ever before.

A sign suspended from the ceiling at the head of the stairs said *Ready to Wear Department, Ladies and Misses.* "I wish to see some children's dresses," Mrs. Thurman told the clerk who advanced to meet them.

"Yes, madam. For this little missie? What kinds did you wish to see, ma'am?"

Mrs. Thurman looked at Jane. "Something rather simple, I think; piqué or linen, if you have it." Jane thought to herself how much nicer *simple* sounded than *plain*. It sounded stylish.

Now and then as she tried on a dress, turning slowly for Mrs. Thurman to see or standing perfectly still while the clerk pinched up the shoulders or took a pleat with her fingers to show how it could be altered to fit, Mrs. Thurman smiled a little. Jane was not quite certain whether she was smiling at her or at something she was thinking about to herself, but she smiled back.

"Would your daughter like a dimity frock for Sunday wear?" The clerk displayed a white dress trimmed with tucks and Valenciennes insertion.

Jane shot an apprehensive glance toward Mrs. Thurman. She hoped she wouldn't mind because the clerk thought she was her daughter. Mrs. Thurman's eyes met hers and she smiled—a smile that spoke as plainly as words, "We have a secret, Jane, haven't we?"

The most wonderful feeling came over Jane, a winged, gliding feeling as if she were sliding down a long smooth snowy hill on a brand-new sled. Her gray eyes shone.

Four dresses had been laid aside on a chair, a blue and white one, a pink plaid gingham, a linen with pink pearl buttons on the pockets, and the beautiful white dimity. "If you'll have them wrapped, we will take them with us." Mrs. Thurman opened her silver-mesh purse. "How much is it, please?"

The clerk figured on a piece of paper. She wet the tip of

her pencil and added the numbers twice. "It comes to exactly twenty-one dollars and seventy-five cents."

Jane almost stopped breathing. Twenty-one dollars! She felt as if a needle had pierced her and let all the happiness escape, like air from a bubble. Twenty-one dollars and seventy-five cents! "Please, ma'am"—she hardly recognized her own voice—"please, I'd rather not have any new dresses."

"Don't you feel well, Jane?" Mrs. Thurman was concerned, solicitous.

"Yes'm, I feel all right. I just don't want new clothes." She turned her eyes away from the beautiful pink and white and blue cascading over the chair. "No'm, I don't really need them, thank you just the same," she insisted unhappily when Mrs. Thurman remonstrated in surprise.

How they left the store Jane could not remember. She only knew that her cheeks felt burning hot and her hands cold, and that the clerk fixed her with a contemptuous stare. Mrs. Thurman stood very tall. "I'm sorry to have put you to so much trouble," she heard Mrs. Thurman apologize. Although the clerk replied that it had been no trouble at all and please come again, Jane sensed the sneer under the polite words.

Time had never gone on such heavy feet as the remainder of that unhappy day. Jane tried to read, but when she got to the bottom of a page she had to read it over again because she did not know what it said. It might as well have been an

75

arithmetic book as *The Wide, Wide World*. When she went outdoors it was as if eyes followed her from the windows of the house. Even the iron girl and boy in the fountain looked aloof.

Aggie kept on with her work when Jane entered the kitchen. Jane sat on the stool. "I'd be pleased to help you, ma'am," she offered timidly. "I'm pretty good at peeling potatoes."

"I've got 'em 'most peeled already." Aggie sounded offended. "And don't *ma'am* me."

"Oh, 'scuse me, ma'am, I mean 'scuse me, Mrs. Simpson." Jane wished she had stayed outdoors, but it was such a long distance from the stool to the door that she remained where she was.

"I can't understand how a little girl would let a lady go to so much trouble as to take a whole morning to go downtown just on her account and then behave so disagreeable. In my day little girls were brought up to know their manners. Not, of course, that there weren't a few ungrateful children even in my time," Aggie conceded darkly.

"Yes, ma'am, I mean yes, Mrs. Simpson." Jane was utterly miserable.

"Nor I'm not to be called Mrs. Simpson, neither," she rebuked Jane. "Aggie's my name and Aggie's what I'm used to being called."

Jane was silent. There was nothing for her to say.

"If you was to ask my advice," Aggie resumed the conversation after she put the potatoes to boil, "I'd tell you to go upstairs and take off that dress so as I can get it washed and ironed before the party. That'll make two times in two days I've had to launder that dress. I certainly hope it's not goin' to be a regular affair, this washin' and ironin'." She thumped an enamel lid on the pan where the tomatoes were cooking.

"Aggie, I'm awfully sorry—I didn't intend—" In spite of her holding her eyes wide open and blinking them fast, the tears would come. A moment later, however, she had pushed the lump down far enough in her throat to say in a voice that sounded almost like her own, "I'll wash it, Aggie. I didn't intend to put you to so much extra trouble. I'm pretty good at ironing, honest I am. And I could wash it too, because it's not really dirty."

"I guess I can do it." Aggie's vexation was evaporating. "Here, want a piece of cold ham? You didn't eat much lunch, I noticed." Jane tried to eat it, to please Aggie, but it had no taste. As soon as she properly could, she slid off the stool and went upstairs to change her dress.

She ate supper in the brown seersucker. Under her eyelashes she caught Mrs. Thurman's eyes upon her in puzzled question. It was as though a wall had thrust up between them, a wall through which they could look, but could not speak.

Jane tried to remember not to say *ma'am*. If Aggie didn't approve of *ma'am,* Mrs. Thurman probably didn't either. Maybe what was good manners for children in a Home was not good manners for other people. After all, she was not in the Home now, she was in a real house and she ought to take pains to act like it.

"Wouldn't you like a white dress to wear to the party?" Mrs. Thurman was gently soothing, as if she were reasoning with a small, sick child. "I could easily telephone to Moore and Mitchell's. Perhaps you did not know that you are having a party. In fact, I planned it as a surprise."

"Yes, ma'am, I mean yes, Mrs. Thurman, I heard you and Aggie talking. I tried not to listen but I couldn't help hearing." Mrs. Thurman looked so troubled it hurt Jane to see her. If only she could explain! But of course she couldn't. "It's kind of you, ma'am, about the dress, but I have all the clothes I need, thank you just the same."

"I see," Mrs. Thurman replied, but Jane knew she did not see.

She had to give herself a good talking-to after she went to bed. "It's not going to hurt you to wear your gingham dress to the party. Plenty of children don't have clothes half as good as you. You ought to be ashamed. Think of the house you're living in like a member of a real family, and yet you complain because you can't have a new dress. I declare it makes me think you're a regular stick-in-the-mud not to appreciate your blessings! Now you just let your conscience be your guide and don't feel put upon when you can't have everything you want." After which plain talking-to, she felt much lighter of heart.

5

THE PARTY

M RS. THURMAN was arranging flowers. Jane would have helped but she was afraid she might be in the way. Throughout the house there was a pleasant stir of anticipation. The open double doors made one long room of the front and back parlors. It certainly was exciting to have a front parlor. The windows reached all the way to the floor, and the varnished shutters were folded back so you could see the lawn and the fountain. At every window there were two sets of curtains, dark red satin ones, draped back to show the silk lining, and long white lace ones with roses and bow-knots in the border. The wallpaper was dark green. The ladies and gentlemen in their gold picture frames looked very refined in old-fashioned clothes.

The furniture was dark and old-fashioned, like that in the back parlor. The carpet was red velvet with a curly pattern of black and green. It was too bad Mrs. Thurman could not have a stylish new upright piano instead of the old square one. Miss Fink said uprights were all the rage; everybody who could afford it was getting a mahogany or quartered-oak upright.

Jane wandered back to the kitchen. Aggie, breathless and red of face from beating eggs and creaming butter and sugar, motioned her to a seat on the high stool. Through the upper part of the window, above the white sash-curtain, Jane could see Abner on the back porch. He was putting chunks of ice into a burlap bag and then hitting the bag with a heavy trowel to crush the ice. Jane knew what that meant, and if she hadn't known, there sat two big ice-cream freezers in plain sight. Abner caught her gaze bent on him. He winked twice and took off his old cap and wiped his forehead. Jane winked back and waved.

"My, I wish I could help," she said.

"You can." Aggie's response was prompt. "Here, wash your hands—clean now, mind you! Grease these cake pans—this for the angel food and those square ones for the devil's food. Mind you get the butter into every corner, else they'll stick. When you finish, take this piece of paper and cut it to fit inside the angel pan, see, like this, and then grease the paper too."

When that was done, there were pans to wash. Aggie gave

her the large yellow bowl in which she had been mixing the devil's food. "You can lick it first, if you want to," she said. "Take this spoon. Don't scrape a hole in the bowl," she joked a little, though she was too busy to have much time for joking.

She was making the icing. "Which'd you ruther have, vanilla or almond flavoring?" She held the egg beater suspended above the platter of downy white icing.

"Almond?" Jane had never tasted it. "Do you think it would be as good with almond? Vanilla's awfully good."

"How'd it be to put almond in the angel icing and vanilla in the devil's food? Then everybody'd have her ruthers."

Jane could not decide which she liked better to scrape, the

yellow bowl with the big wooden spoon where the cake batter had been mixed, or the deep white platter sticky with boiled sugar syrup and egg whites whipped to a feathery lightness and flavored with vanilla. The cake batter was more substantial, your tongue could discover more things in it—butter and sugar, chocolate, smooth-sifted flour, cream and flavoring— but the icing melted on your tongue like snowflakes of sweetness and left you feeling happier than if you lived in a candy shop. Fortunately she did not have to make a choice, for Aggie took it for granted that she would scrape both before she put them into the round granite dishpan to wash.

After the angel food cake was slipped into the oven, Jane had to sit very quiet on the stool and Abner was not allowed to enter the kitchen, although he needed more salt to make the ice melt. A jar, said Aggie, would make the cake fall. She would have no stumping about on her kitchen floor or opening and shutting of doors until the cake was safely out. While they waited, Aggie rolled lemons to make them soft so all the juice would squeeze out for lemonade. Two whole dozen, Jane counted.

"That's a lot of lemons," she said.

"Not one too many," Aggie countered. "You mark my words, they'll drink it all. And while we're on the subject, there'll be ice cream enough for everybody to have seconds. It's peach. They'll want two helpings and they'll take it if you urge 'em a trifle. You mustn't forget. There's plenty of cake for everybody to eat as much as she likes, one piece of angel and one of devil's to start with, and more of both in the kitchen."

Jane closed her eyes for a clearer foretaste of the afternoon's promised bliss. Suddenly she opened them wide. "Aggie," she queried anxiously, "isn't this party costing Mrs. Thurman a lot of money?"

"No, I wouldn't say so. All it takes is butter and eggs and cream, and they're plentifully cheap at this season of the year. She always buys her sugar in such quantity it comes cheaper. And peaches and lemons— No, I wouldn't call this a dear party."

They ate a cold snack at noon, because the dining room was ready for the party. The table had been stretched out almost as long as the one at the orphanage, and covered with a white cloth that practically touched the floor on both sides. In the center stood a deep oval bowl (it looked like silver, but Jane didn't suppose it really was), filled with sprays of blue larkspur and white stock and pink and white pinks. Even from the doorway she could smell the spicy stock and pinks. The larkspur had no smell at all.

Twenty places were laid, each with a fork and spoon and a fringed tissue-paper cylinder, pink and blue and yellow, beside a folded linen napkin. Favors, Mrs. Thurman explained, when she saw Jane inspecting them, her hands behind her back.

"I should have known." Jane sighed with satisfaction. "I've read about them in books."

They ate the snack in the kitchen, all except Abner, who preferred the back porch where there was a breeze. No one ate much. Jane had sampled the cake batter and icing too liberally to have an appetite, and Mrs. Thurman and Aggie both declared themselves too excited to be hungry. Jane thought to herself that it was strange she did not feel excited. She felt very calm and collected. She felt as if she were not herself at all, but some other girl looking with her eyes and thinking with her mind.

Mrs. Thurman went to her room to lie down for a few minutes, but Jane dressed immediately. She rubbed her high shoes until they shone, the sides and back as well as the toes. She pulled up her long stockings until the ribs were straight lines, and fastened the hose supporters tight. Miss Fink maintained that there wasn't anything like wrinkles in a girl's stockings to take away her style. She maneuvered the freshly starched blue gingham carefully over her head and stood before the mirror to make sure her petticoat did not show.

Jane gazed with astonished pleasure when Mrs. Thurman appeared in the parlor. "You look lovely, Mrs. Thurman." Her eyes seconded the enthusiasm that spoke in her voice. "I know it's not polite to talk about people's clothes, but you look exactly like a fashion-book picture. I wish Miss Fink could lay eyes on you." Suddenly self-conscious and shy, she added in a subdued tone, "I hope you'll 'scuse me please for mentioning your dress."

"I'm glad you like it." Mrs. Thurman glanced down at her shell-pink voile, with its belt of twisted satin. "I was hoping you would. And you look as neat and fresh as if you had just stepped out of a bandbox."

Jane was pleased to be complimented.

"I wonder if you wouldn't like to wear a rosebud on your shoulder," Mrs. Thurman suggested. Jane stood very still, scarcely breathing, holding her head to one side—the wet comb marks were still showing in her brown hair—while the flower was pinned on. "There," Mrs. Thurman surveyed the blue gingham shoulder where the rosebud nestled. "Now everybody will be able to see who the hostess is."

It seemed a long wait until half-past two o'clock. Jane would have worried for fear nobody would come—they might forget or think it was tomorrow or their mothers mightn't let them —but Mrs. Thurman appeared so much at ease that Jane took her cue from her. If they just knew about the lemonade and peach ice cream and two kinds of cake with icing on, wild elephants couldn't keep them away.

The guests began to arrive, some on foot and others in

carriages which wheeled leisurely around and went jogging off again. Mrs. Thurman stood beside Jane to introduce the guests—India Maud Meadows and Louise Craig, Florence and Alice Andrews, Cissie Matthews, who greeted Jane like an old friend, Mary Bryden, Sarah Williams, Annabelle Jones, Emily Welch, Jean Peirce, and all the others. They sat primly erect, skirts spread wide on the green velvet sofa and dark old chairs. They talked as politely to each other as if they were their own mothers and aunts.

When the last guest had arrived, panting and with hair-ribbons askew because she had run most of the way, Mrs. Thurman excused herself. She might be needed in the kitchen, she said. They might play games in the house or on the lawn, as they preferred. If they enjoyed paper-and-pencil games, Jane would supply them with pencils and foolscap.

In certain ways Jane felt more sure of herself after Mrs. Thurman's departure. It was harder to think of things to say while she was there, because you kept thinking about your manners. And as everyone knows, too much thinking about manners often keeps people from becoming friends.

"Would you like to play charades?" she asked. There was silence. Some guests looked at Jane, some at each other. "Or riddles, like 'On top of a hill there's a mill, and under the mill there's a walk, and under the walk there's a key; what is it?'"

The silence spread and grew chilly. The guests were all looking at her. She had almost forgotten about the blue gingham, but now she remembered. She noticed that every girl, every single one, was wearing a white dress; yes, and a silk sash tied around her waist.

"Let's have somebody leave the room and we hide something and then she comes back and guesses where it's hidden." Jane tried to sound as if what she was proposing were the most fun in the world.

Nobody answered. There was no friendliness, no flicker of kindness in the faces confronting her. They stared as if she were quite different from themselves and they were too well brought up to have anything to do with her. Jane felt herself turning red—not just her face, but her ears and neck. She could feel the burning color begin to move down her body. She held herself steady, although she could hardly keep her voice from wavering.

"Would you like to play drop-the-handkerchief outdoors?"

Silence answered her. Nineteen pairs of eyes—blue, brown, hazel-colored—stared at her without blinking. For a moment Jane was frightened. Frightened and helpless. It was as though she were trapped in a solid piece of glass like the little sheep inside Matron's paperweight. She was not herself any longer, she was not Jane Douglas. She was a person to be stared at. The girls would go away and make fun of her behind her

back. They would talk about her and make fun of her blue dress and her short hair.

Unexpectedly, something within her boiled up, seethed and bubbled, burst into flame like an exploding rocket. She threw back her head and stamped her foot. Her gray eyes were blazing.

"I'm going out to the stable and play pirate chief," she announced loudly. "It's the most exciting game in the world. It's the kind that boys play when they won't let girls play with them. If anyone wants to play with me, come along. If you don't, you can just sit here forever for all I care!"

There was a stir, a shuffling of black patent-leather slippers on the thick red carpet, a swishing of starched dimity and organdy and crisp taffeta sashes. The set faces relaxed; the eyes blinked.

Jane was quick to sense her advantage. "I'll explain about the game." It was no longer necessary to talk loudly, because everybody was paying attention. "There's a pirate chief and his band. They have to be awfully daring and venturesome because if they're not, they get caught and—" She paused dramatically. She was beginning to feel gay and excited and venturesome herself. But she mustn't let herself go; she had to keep her head. She had to think quickly, for she did not know what would happen to the pirates if they got caught. It was a new game that she was making up as she went along. "They have to pay a forfeit."

"Is that all there is to it? I thought it was something special. I've played lots of games like that." Cissie was superior, bored.

Others looked as if they were not particularly interested in pirate chief after all. Cissie's air of disdain had made an impression.

"Not like this one, you haven't!" Jane maintained stoutly. She braced herself to keep her courage from slipping. She would fight to the end for her rights. She would not let Cissie take the party away from her; it wasn't Cissie's party, it was her own. Mrs. Thurman was giving it for her, Jane Douglas. She would not let Cissie have her way with the party and make Jane feel left out.

"Besides the pirates there's a rich family that has a box of treasure and a beautiful daughter," she continued, looking straight at Cissie.

"That sounds spiffy!" The deep, booming voice was India Maud's. She leaned forward eagerly from the sofa. "Does the pirate chief try to steal the treasure?"

The question served like a heady tonic. Jane's mind began to work faster and faster, more and more confidently. "Not just the treasure." She was speaking to India Maud, but she noted out of the corner of her eye that the others were all waiting to hear the answer too. "He tries to steal the daughter!

He's in love with her."

"Does he get her?" This from Cissie, whose fancy was snared by the beauteous daughter.

India Maud turned upon her. "That's what the game is about, silly! I should think you could figure out that much for yourself." She walked over to Jane. "I'm going to be the girl's father that fights to protect her. Jane, you can be the pirate chief."

"Let's not have it her father," objected Annabelle. "Fathers are too old. Let's have it a young man she's engaged to."

"Suits me," said India Maud. "I don't care who he is just so I'm him."

"I'll be the daughter," volunteered Cissie, quite carried away by enthusiasm now that India Maud and Annabelle approved the game.

"You? Don't be silly, Cissie. You're too big. You're half a head taller than I am. How'd it look to have the daughter bigger than the man that protects her?" There was no denying the soundness of India Maud's reasoning. "Mary'd make a good daughter. You can be the mother, Cissie." Mary, shy and small and beaming with pleasure, lined up beside her champion.

"Now, Jane, you and I'll choose the ones we want on our sides." India Maud was like a general marshaling his staff.

Deeply grateful to India Maud though she was, Jane was

93

not quite willing to have her take charge. "Don't you think, India Maud," she proposed tactfully, "that we might let them choose which side they'd rather be on—pirates or protectors?"

"When everybody's running and hiding, how can we tell which are pirates?" questioned practical Sarah Williams. "I'll be sure to forget who is what."

"Pirates," commanded Jane, "take off your hair ribbons and leave them in the parlor."

"My sash too," said Florence, "and yours, Alice. Remember what mamma said about being careful."

Similar injunctions must have been issued by other parents, for nineteen sashes were hastily draped over the sofa and outspread on chair backs. The parlor resembled a giant, rainbow-colored spider web.

"You didn't say what the forfeit is," Beth Topping reminded Jane.

For the fraction of a minute Jane was at a loss. While she groped hastily through her mind, her eyes focused on something outside the window—the fountain. Four silvery jets were arching through the shallow shade to break in sparkling spray against the iron umbrella. "The losers must take their shoes and stockings off and stick their feet into the fountain." She proclaimed the forfeit like a judge. Everybody giggled.

They were in the stable when India Maud groaned, "This dress! I forgot, I can't play!" Her manner was calamitous

There was a chorus of questions and protests. "Angeline" (during the course of the afternoon Jane learned that India Maud called her mother and father by their first names, Angeline and George)—"Angeline wouldn't let me wear it unless I promised to play only sit-down games. She bought it in Chicago. It's real China silk and the French knots are hand-embroidered."

If India Maud couldn't play, no one else would. Jane summoned her resources. "I'll lend you a patched dress. It won't matter what you do to that."

Rover came bouncing across the lawn to join them, his elderly legs flying with youthful eagerness. Reluctantly, and only because there seemed no other solution, Jane escorted him to the kitchen to stay with Aggie. Neither pirates nor protectors were willing to risk betrayal of their hiding places by a dog, even when the dog was as anxious to please as Rover.

The game proved even more fun than Jane had hoped. There were advances and retreats, strategies, giggles, whispered warnings and shouted threats. The pirates were almost captured as they crouched behind the gooseberry bushes in the vegetable garden; and the protectors barely escaped with the treasure from the snowball bushes and bridal wreath hedge. The beautiful daughter was lost and won, won and lost again. Once the pirates were driven into ambush against the iron fence and would have been taken prisoners, but with a rallying shout the chief led the harassed crew in a break for the fountain and freedom.

Whose the ultimate victory would have been was not known, for late in the afternoon, as the protectors gathered breath under the hedge and took counsel for their next strategy, Aggie summoned them with a little bell. They went streaming upstairs to wash their hands and streamed hastily down again. They did not delay for sashes and ribbons, but fell upon the goblets of lemonade like seamen long marooned on a water-famished isle. When Mrs. Thurman replenished the glasses from a tall pitcher, beaded with moisture and tinkling with ice, she set a fresh sprig of mint afloat in each goblet.

When, last of all, she bent to refill Jane's glass, Jane whispered in her ear, "How did you ever make the lemonade turn pink? It's as pretty as circus lemonade!"

"Cinnamon drops!" came the lightly whispered response. Yes, now Jane could taste the cinnamon though before she had noticed only the flavor of mint leaves in the ice-cold, sour-sweet lemonade.

India Maud did not wait for the others. "Angeline says it's all right to begin as soon as the people next to you have their refreshments." She slid a spoonful of ice cream into her mouth.

The chunks of frozen peach made pale pink splotches in

the creamy mound. It looked so pretty that for a moment Jane was content just to look at it. And no wonder you had to have a fork to eat the cake! The devil's food layer cake was so rich that it almost crumbled to pieces. The angel food held up better because it was stiffer. She let her tongue linger on the icing to get the full savor of the almond flavoring. It tasted sweet and fancy, but not so satisfying as vanilla.

When the last spoon had been laid down in the last empty sauce dish and the last fork brought to rest on the last gold-rimmed plate, Aggie helped Mrs. Thurman retie the sashes and furbish up the rumpled dresses. Mary Bryden and flaxen-haired Beth Topping looked almost as spick-and-span as they had upon arrival.

Then everybody politely thanked Mrs. Thurman for a pleasant afternoon and told Jane what a perfectly scrumptious party it had been. On foot or in carriages, as they had come, the guests set off under the lengthening shadows of the oak and maple trees. All except India Maud. She lingered. Aggie had helped her with the China silk dress, but her long curls still looked like untidily frayed yellow corn-silk.

"Angeline makes a fuss if I get messed up," she remarked, twisting the end of a curl around a finger. "Usually I slide in through the back door so she won't see me. Say, Jane," changing the subject, "will you come to my house to dinner tomorrow? I've got a Shetland pony and a work-bench in the basement with real tools."

Jane looked toward Mrs. Thurman. "That is kind of you, India Maud," replied Mrs. Thurman, "but it may not be convenient for your mother. Don't you think it would be better to wait a few days?"

"Any day's all right," she asserted. "I always get my own way. If I can't get it from Angeline, I go to George. They almost never both say no at the same time."

Jane helped Mrs. Thurman pick up the napkins and the torn paper favors. "Did you enjoy your party?" Mrs. Thurman inquired.

"Did I!" Jane's tone left no room for doubt. "Why, Mrs. Thurman, when I think that I've lived all my life without knowing how wonderful it is to have a party, I guess I've been a regular stick-in-the-mud!" She brushed the scraps of paper into a heap and made two neat piles of the napkins.

Her face grew sober. "Are you sure you didn't have to lay out a lot of money for refreshments, Mrs. Thurman? Aggie said not, but Matron always says cream and lemons and sugar come dear. I could help pay. I've got a dollar and ten cents."

"Thank you, Jane, but Aggie spoke the truth. Lemons and cream are plentiful in July. You may need your money later. And now perhaps Aggie would like your help with the dishes."

Aggie was going to church after supper to see stereopticon

views. She said that last winter a missionary had shown stere-opticon scenes of China. "It's a good thing I was never a missionary to China," she told Jane. "I couldn't stand doin' without potatoes. Rice is all right in rice pudding, and now and then steamed with butter and cream and brown sugar; but give me potatoes any day." Jane agreed that dinner wouldn't be dinner without potatoes, preferably mashed.

"Aggie, what country do gypsies come from?" Jane was drying the plates.

Aggie had never thought about it, but she supposed Egypt. Probably they had run away, like the children of Israel. "But they didn't run away, Aggie; they *escaped*, don't you remember?" Jane was disturbed by Aggie's mistake about the Bible until she happened to notice her expression. Aggie was joking.

"Whatever made you think of gypsies?" she wanted to know. "They're a triflin' lot. Light-fingered, too."

Jane had thought she might tell Aggie about the gypsy princess, but now she changed her mind. Aggie wasn't really acquainted with a gypsy, the way Jane was. She would think Jane's gypsy was like all the others. Jane couldn't bear to have Aggie call the princess trifling, nor the black-eyed, warm-fingered baby. She wouldn't mention them to Aggie. She'd keep them to herself to remember.

Matron had given her two stamped envelopes and sheets of paper. Jane wrote a letter after supper. She explained about

Mrs. Thurman's having to live in an old house with old furniture. Did Matron think she ought to tell her about the infirmary anyhow?

Matron's reply came on a postal card. "Use your own judgment about the i.," she said. "Remember not to make extra
work for anybody and be a good girl." Everybody at the Home
was well, but Miss Fink had broken her spectacles.

🐜 🐜 🐜 6 🐜 🐜 🐜

DINNER AT INDIA MAUD'S

ALICE WHITE was coming to sew, and she might as well make something for Jane too. Which dress would she like to wear to India Maud's? There was pink striped gingham, and light blue piqué. There was yellow chambray, with lace for trimming. (Mrs. Thurman called it Irish crochet, but it was different from the lace Matron and Miss Fink crocheted.) And to make Jane's thoughts dance even faster with delight, there was white organdy with a pink taffeta sash.

"Oh, Mrs. Thurman, even when I pinch myself and the pinch hurts, I can't believe I'm awake!" Jane hopped up and down on one foot and attempted to hold the other clasped in both hands. "Even if I were a floorwalker's daughter in a big store I wouldn't dare to wish for all this!"

She decided, not without an effort of will, to have the ging-ham made first. Life in the orphanage had taught her, among other things, that what you wish for is not always what you ought to have. Matron set a high value on common sense, and common sense would never, by any stretch of reasoning, sanction a fancy dress to ride a Shetland pony or to hammer and saw at a work-bench.

Alice White arrived early. Jane, who had associated her name with the "Sweet Alice" of the old song, thought she would be a fair young girl. She was disappointed to see a gaunt woman with a plain face. Alice White and Aggie had known each other always, it seemed. They had gone to school together and lived across the street from each other, and Alice White had "stood up" with Aggie and Abner when they were married. Jane sat on the high stool while they chatted over the hot coffee and sugared coffee-cake which Aggie set out on a corner of the kitchen table. She munched a piece with them, to be sociable.

"How's Clarence? What's he up to now?" inquired Aggie, stirring the cream and sugar round and round in her cup.

Alice White laughed, her plain face breaking into a thousand kindly wrinkles. "You'd never guess, Aggie. He's raisin' Belgian hares, about two hundred of 'em. He expects to clear a tidy sum."

"Belgian hares? D'you mean rabbits, Alice?"

Alice White took a second piece of cake. "They're very special rabbits, somethin' extry fine. He figgers that if he gets fifty cents a skin and they keep multiplyin' the way they do, you know, he can stop work and live on the profits."

"Who in thunder would pay half a dollar for a rabbit skin? Abner fetches 'em in in huntin' season, and they ain't a mortal thing you can do with 'em. Nobody with gumption is going to throw away good money on rabbit skins."

"Yes, they do, Aggie." Superiority and sly amusement mingled in Alice White's voice. "They buy these rabbit skins —not the plain ones, I grant you, but these fancy Belgian hare ones—to make sealskin coats. Sealskin was all the go last winter, and Clarence figgers on it again this winter. I shouldn't be at all surprised" (the air of importance with which she imparted the information impressed Jane), "no, not at all surprised, if Clarence makes money out of this venture."

"It would be the first time he ever did!" Aggie emphasized her doubts with a thump of the coffeepot. "All I can say is I'm glad I'm not his wife. I 'spose she takes care of the rabbits?"

"He lends a hand when he's not switchin'." Noting Jane's puzzled frown, Alice White explained, "My brother Clarence is a switchman on the Big Four." She pushed her empty cup aside. "I'd better get to work."

An upstairs room had been made ready, the bed pushed against the wall and the leaves of the walnut side table extended for a cutting table. In the breeze between the windows stood a sewing machine. Aggie flecked off an imaginary speck of dust before she lifted the box-like hood.

"Which one you goin' to wear to India Maud's house?" she asked Jane.

"The pink gingham." She hoped Aggie would approve.

"That's sensible," was Aggie's comment. "Maybe you can teach India Maud some sense. Her mother dresses her like a circus performer or one of them ballet toe-dancers." Aggie pronounced it *ballot,* as did Jane, who knew the word only from reading.

Jane could not help thinking it would be fun to dress like a ballet dancer—at least sometimes.

Aggie snorted. "Her mother's afraid somebody'll remember that before she married the banker's son she waited table in her ma's boarding house. She dresses herself fit to kill, and India Maud too. There's no disgrace in runnin' a boarding house, but she's ashamed of it." Aggie's mouth puckered in disapproval just like Matron's. "A foolish woman," Aggie passed judgment upon Mrs. Meadows. "I feel sorry for George Meadows now that he's older and got some sense."

Jane felt uncomfortable. She liked India Maud, and this criticizing of her mother seemed a reflection on India Maud. She was glad when Mrs. Thurman's step in the hall brought a change of subject.

Alice White hooked her silver-rimmed spectacles over her

ears and laid needles and thimble on the machine. She unfolded her tape measure. "Let's see how big you are, Janie. Do
you want I should allow room to grow, Mrs. Thurman?"

As if she read the intense wish written in Jane's mind, Mrs.
Thurman said no. "Make the hems deep enough to let out,
but otherwise we'll have the dresses to size now."

Jane stretched out her arm to be measured. "This'll be the
first time I ever had a new dress that wasn't too big," she
informed them gaily. "That brown seersucker was so big that
Sammy Brown—he lives in the Home and he likes to tease—
Sammy said he couldn't tell whether it was me or Miss Fink
walking around inside it. Of course he didn't let Miss Fink
hear." She must not let them think Sammy had no manners.

Alice White needed no pattern. From a smooth piece of
brown wrapping paper that Jane fetched from the kitchen,
she cut a yoke which she held to Jane's back and shoulders,
trimming the edges until it was the right size. Then she spread
the pink gingham on the table, surveyed first Jane over the
top of her silver-bowed spectacles, and then the gingham,
and began to cut. The scissors hummed as they sheared
through the pink cloth. Jane's thoughts sang with the scissors.
Wasn't it lucky for her that Alice White had come to sew
while she was visiting? Wasn't it lucky that Mrs. Thurman
had all that dress goods? Enough to make four dresses, and
not a single one of them brown! She must have bought the

silk sash special.

A day or two later Abner hitched old Polly to take Jane to India Maud's. It was two miles, Mrs. Thurman said; much too far to walk on such a hot day.

"There's the Meaders' place." Abner pointed with the buggy whip to a new house, built of yellow brick, with white columns in front and large plate glass windows. It looked so imposing that Jane almost wished she had not been invited. She waited on the sidewalk while Abner turned the horse around and drove off, the black-topped surrey now in flickering shade, now in bright sunshine. There was no help for it; she could not stand forever on the corner, India Maud was expecting her. Of course she'd have a good time, once she was inside the house.

It seemed a long time after she punched the doorbell before she heard any sounds. She hoped India Maud would be the one to answer the bell. It was a lady, however, who stood in the narrow crack looking down at her. She did not look as if she was expecting anybody, for she had on a purple kimono.

"I'm Jane Douglas." Even to herself her voice sounded weak.

The lady looked Jane up and down, slowly.

"I've come to play with India Maud. She asked me to," explained Jane. She kept her feet planted solidly on the rubber door mat, though she longed to face about and run away. If only India Maud would come!

And India Maud did come, flying around the corner of the house to hurl herself at Jane. "Hello, Jane," she cried breathlessly. "I've been expecting you for ever so long. Angeline,

this is Jane. Come on, we'll go to the stable. I've been currying Daisy. I'll let you ride her if you want to." She hooked her arm in Jane's and hurried her off the porch. The lady shut the door with a slight bang.

Daisy was the first Shetland pony Jane had ever petted. She let her head rest on Jane's shoulder as contentedly as if they had always been friends, but even while Jane stroked the white star on her forehead and listened to India Maud tell what fun they would have after dinner when they went driving all by themselves to Finfrock's drugstore for an ice-cream soda, Jane could not help remembering how India Maud's mother had looked at her. It made her feel heavy inside her mind, as if she had done something wrong and were waiting to be scolded.

"Don't be a stick-in-the-mud!" she warned herself. "India Maud's trying to give you a good time." She must not let her notice how she felt. "Can you harness Daisy yourself?" Jane forced herself to speak cheerfully.

"Of course," said India Maud complacently. "I'll show you." She dragged out the harness. "Hold this. Look—" but with an impudent sidesweep the innocent-looking Daisy had tossed the bridle to the floor.

Jane laughed. "She has a mind of her own. I like ponies with minds of their own, don't you, India Maud? They're more like people."

"She's stubborn, all right. Even George has a hard time hitching her when she's made up her mind not to. Sometimes she stops stock-still in the middle of the road and I have to get out and pull her." India Maud was beginning to feel proud of Daisy's obstinacy.

They curried her flanks until she shone like brown satin, and combed and brushed her mane and tail, and braided her forelock and tied it out of her eyes. They placed the harness in readiness, to use the moment dinner was finished. They would bring some lumps of sugar from the table to put Daisy in a pliable mood. India Maud said she would show Jane how to drive, but she'd have to keep the reins herself on Main Street because it took a good driver to weave in and out among so many buggies.

Nora called them to dinner. While Jane dried her hands on a kitchen towel, India Maud dashed upstairs to put on a hair ribbon. "I'll be right back," she promised, stopping to shine the toes of her shoes on the back of her stockings. "You just go into the hall and wait for me."

Mrs. Meadows was at the telephone. Jane did not know whether Mrs. Meadows heard her come in, but she could not help hearing what Mrs. Meadows said. The first words made no impression on her, but there followed phrases that seared like burning coals. It was not she, not Jane Douglas, of whom the shameful words were said. It was someone else, someone who was helpless to move or speak because she could not wake herself from a dreadful dream. She wanted to scream, she wanted to run away from the shame of the dream, but she could not move.

"No, I'm afraid India Maud will miss the tableaux. She's invited somebody here—a waif or beggar from an asylum who's staying at Cora Thurman's.—No, you know how India Maud is; she'd refuse to leave her."

Jane felt smothered, choking hot and at the same time cold

and heavy as stone. She clenched her fists and set her teeth. It was not true; she was not a beggar, she was no more a beggar than Mrs. Meadows. She worked to pay her way at the orphanage. She had never begged in her whole life.

India Maud was standing in the doorway, looking at her. Jane did not know whether India Maud had heard or not. With an effort she summoned her voice. "Good-bye, India Maud," she said. She walked straight toward the door.

India Maud planted herself in the door to bar the way. "But we haven't had dinner! Don't go, Jane," she begged. "Nora made something special because I asked her to, for you. Please stay, Jane."

Jane pulled her hand free. "I can't stay." Her voice sounded loud, but she couldn't help it.

India Maud caught at her again. "I'll cry if you go, Jane. I can't bear it if you go. I'll cry and cry." There was a real sob in her voice. "Nora made blancmange with chocolate sauce specially on your account. Please stay, Jane."

Jane moved as if she were propelled by machinery. She couldn't have stopped if she had wanted to. When she reached the sidewalk her hands were still clenched tight, her jaw still set and stiff. Her face burned like fire. She could scarcely see the bricks in the sidewalk because the tears kept coming faster than she could wink them away. Now and then she stumbled over an uneven place. With the stumbling, however, her

mind seemed gradually to jolt itself back into thinking again.
She turned down a side street so she would not meet anyone.

If only she had a ticket back to the orphanage! If only she
could earn enough money for one! But Abner and Aggie did
Mrs. Thurman's work; she did not need anyone else. If only
a lady in the neighborhood had a baby that Jane might take
care of while the lady went downtown! But Jane did not even
know which families had babies. Oh, why hadn't Mrs. Scott
invited her to Cherry Valley before Matron thought of sending her to Danbury!

It was more than an hour later when she reached the gray
brick house, quiet and cool under the great old trees. She
wished there wouldn't be anyone on the side porch, but there
was. Mrs. Thurman was sewing lace on the collar and cuffs
of Jane's yellow dress. At the sound of Jane's step on the gravel
driveway she looked up in surprise. "Are you back so soon,
Jane? Did you—did something—" She did not finish the
question.

Jane stood on the top step. She hoped Mrs. Thurman would
not look at her. She wished she could get into the house and
upstairs before Mrs. Thurman looked up again. She was
threading a needle, holding it high to get a better light. The
needle must have been very small, because it took so long to
thread it. Jane stood still. She did not know what else to do.

"You must be hot and tired." Mrs. Thurman's voice was

gentle. 'Why don't you go to your room, Jane, and cool your face with cold water? It's a hot day to walk such a long distance. While you're cooling off, I'll get some lunch. Aggie made floating island and we saved some for you, because you like it so much."

"Yes, ma'am." Jane tried to say *thank you,* but the words stuck in her throat.

Before she had reached the top of the stairs, the tears broke forth. She closed the bathroom door and stuffed the end of a towel into her mouth so nobody would hear her cry. She scolded herself. "What's the matter with you? What are you crying about?" At which the tears burst forth afresh, for there was plenty of reason for her crying, and she knew it.

She tried again, this time more gently, to reason with herself. "You mustn't let a mean stuck-up lady make you feel bad," she told herself. "Keep your chin up and let your conscience be your guide. Remember what Miss Fink says: it's no good crying over spilled milk. It wasn't you that spilled it anyhow. You didn't do anything bad. You didn't even talk back."

The sobs abated. She splashed her face with cold water and mopped it dry with a towel. She wet her hair and combed it smooth. "Now don't you make Mrs. Thurman feel bad, she's so nice to you. She can't help what happened. It's not true what Mrs. Meadows said anyhow; you know it's not. Don't be a stick-in-the-mud, Jane Douglas."

A tray awaited her on the porch. Though sandwiches usually made her feel picnicky, today it was as if a walnut shell
were lodged in her throat and she could hardly swallow. By the
time she came to the yellow and white floating island, however,
tasting deliciously of cream and vanilla, and alternately smooth
to the tongue and fluffy as a cloud, she felt more like herself.

"That was good," she told Mrs. Thurman. "It's almost
better than ice cream. And you're awfully nice to sew the lace
on my dress. I wish I could help."

"Would you like to pull out the basting threads?" Jane
knew from the quick way Mrs. Thurman accepted her offer
that she was pleased to have her help.

For a time they worked in silence. It was pleasant on the
porch, with a breeze rustling through the trees and making
the sunlight ripple across the grass. Rover lumbered from the
darkened hall to lie on the floor between them, his eyes filmed
with sleep, the tip of his pink tongue visible between his
pointed white teeth.

"You have not said much about the James Ballard Home,"
Mrs. Thurman remarked after a while. "I should like to know
more about it."

"Yes, ma'am," said Jane. "What would you like to know?"

"Whatever you'd like to tell." She was beginning on the
second cuff. "Are there many children of your age?"

"Only some boys," answered Jane. "There were two girls older than I am, but their father married again and they went home to live. Ever since, I've been the oldest girl. Lula and Hazel are next oldest, but I'm almost half a year older than Lula. I help take care of the babies."

"Are there many to take care of?"

"Sometimes, but sometimes they get adopted. I'm 'fraid somebody'll adopt Peter while I'm gone. He's my favorite, he's so little and his hair is curly and he's just full of mischief. Not real badness, you know, but things like running off. Once he got into the cellar where the cabbage and potatoes are stored, and it took me the longest time to find him. He was happy I found him, because it was dark down there and he couldn't get out."

Jane scratched Rover's ears. She had finished pulling the bastings. She liked sitting on the porch with Mrs. Thurman as if they had known each other ever and ever so long. "I wish Miss Fink could see your front parlor, Mrs. Thurman," she said, leaning back comfortably in her chair. "She'd love those red satin curtains."

"Is she your teacher?"

"Oh, my, no!" Jane was amused at the thought of Miss Fink's teaching school. "She's in the nursery. It was she gave me the red pocketbook. She never tells Matron when I read in bed."

Mrs. Thurman smiled. "So that's a failing of yours! It's one of mine too. Does anyone help you and Miss Fink?"

"We don't really need help. Mostly, that is. Of course if someone gets sick—bad sick, I mean—it's different. They all have to sleep in the same room, and if one gets pneumonia or measles or anything, some of the others are almost sure to catch it. That's because the orphanage doesn't have enough money to build an infirmary—" She caught herself. She mustn't make Mrs. Thurman sorry about the infirmary when she couldn't afford the money for it. "Oh, we manage to get on," she hastened to add, minimizing the difficulty. "Don't you worry about us, Mrs. Thurman. We'll get along all right."

Mrs. Thurman held up the yellow dress. "Would you ask Alice White if it needs another buttonhole? While you're upstairs, you might put the dress on and let me see how it looks."

When Jane came down a few minutes later she heard voices and saw the back of a man in a gray alpaca suit. He was holding a straw hat behind him. She hesitated, but Mrs. Thurman motioned her to join them. Then Jane saw that India Maud was with the man, hanging to his arm.

"Here is Jane now." Mrs. Thurman took Jane's hand in hers. "Jane, this is Mr. Meadows."

"How do you do, sir," said Jane. "Hello, India Maud." The memory of Mrs. Meadows woke aching and burning within her, making her feel ill at ease. She was glad Mrs. Thurman kept hold of her hand.

India Maud lifted a tear-swollen face. "Hello, Jane." She sniffled and her voice sounded as if she had a cold. "George has come to see if you won't come to my house."

Jane felt sorry for India Maud, her nose and eyes were so puffed up and red. She looked as if she had cried and cried. But she could not say yes. She shook her head to say no.

"George," insisted India Maud, and it sounded as if she might at any moment weep again, "George, you promised you'd persuade her."

Mr. Meadows' face was perspiring and shiny. He looked almost as unhappy as India Maud.

"Tell Jane what you told me, George," suggested Mrs. Thurman. She drew Jane closer and slipped her arm through hers.

He took out a big white handkerchief and wiped his forehead. His eyes were almost as blue as India Maud's. "I wish you wouldn't hold India Maud responsible for what happened, Jane," he began, as if uncertain what to say. "She couldn't help the misunderstanding. She came all the way down to the bank to get me without her dinner, and she's hardly stopped crying since."

India Maud nodded violently to confirm his statement. "That's so, Jane, and I can hardly keep from doing it right now." As a matter of fact, however, she looked more cheerful. She was evidently confident of her father's ability to make things come out the way she wished.

Jane looked from Mr. Meadows' worried face to India Maud's tear-stained one, and back again to his. "I'd like to, Mr. Meadows"—she wished he had not asked her—"honest I would, but I can't." She met his eyes squarely.

He took out his handkerchief again and mopped his face. "Can't you persuade her, Cora?" He seemed almost to plead. "You know how Angeline is. She won't hurt Jane's feelings again. She said she wouldn't, didn't she, India Maud? Sometimes she hurts our feelings too, doesn't she, India Maud? It's because she's so nervous and her health's delicate. You mustn't pay any attention when she says things like that, Jane. It's just her delicate health that makes her do it."

"This is something Jane must decide for herself." Mrs. Thurman's fingers gave Jane's an encouraging squeeze. "She is the only one who can decide what is right."

Jane was deeply grateful to her for understanding how things were. She felt that she could never, never go to Mrs. Meadows' house again, not if she lived to be a hundred years old and Mrs. Meadows herself got down on her bended knees to invite her. Before she could reply, however, India Maud had let go of her father and planted herself directly before her.

"Please say yes, Jane; *please!* I like you ever and ever so much. I want you for my best friend. I want us to be friends for ever and ever."

Something within Jane melted, something that had remained like a tight knot in her mind all afternoon even when she thought she had forgotten it, something hard and unyielding and hurtful. It melted like a cold snowflake at the touch of a warm hand. India Maud wanted her to be her best friend. Never in Jane's whole life had anybody asked her to be her best friend.

Jane's gray eyes looked into India Maud's blue ones and found there a friend, honest and true. "Yes, India Maud. Yes, Mr. Meadows," she answered. Her voice was low, but it rang clear.

India Maud flung herself upon Jane and hugged her. "Oh, Jane, I'm so glad." She spoke between laughing and crying. "You can't think how glad I am! We'll go right now. George will hitch Daisy and we'll go to the drugstore and get a soda water and you can drive every step of the way there and every step of the way back."

"Could I come some other day, India Maud? I'm helping Mrs. Thurman now."

"Tomorrow?" India Maud pressed, anxious, urgent.

"A week from tomorrow, perhaps," suggested Mrs. Thurman. "Alice White needs Jane to try on dresses."

"A week from tomorrow it is, then." Mr. Meadows put out his hand and took Jane's small tense one in his big friendly grasp. "You're a good sport, Jane," he said. "I'm glad you and India Maud are going to keep on being friends."

"I'm glad too," answered Jane.

After the Meadows' carriage had driven down the driveway, Mrs. Thurman put both hands on Jane's shoulders. Then she took one hand off and lifted Jane's face so that she could look straight down into her eyes. "It is good blood that flows in your veins, Jane Douglas," she said. She kissed her lightly on the forehead.

"Now upstairs with you, young lady, and out of that yellow dress before Alice White catches us!" She gave Jane a little push. "Alice White would scold us both if she knew I let you wear it before it was pressed."

Jane laughed out loud. She couldn't help it, she felt so happy. "I won't let her see me!" she called back as she ran up the stairs, two steps at a time.

7

A LETTER FROM MATRON

CISSIE came over to invite Jane to her house. Florence and Alice Andrews were coming, and Louise Craig. They were going to make cardboard streetcars, and in the evening there would be a streetcar parade in front of Emily Welch's house on Prairie Avenue. Emily had telephoned Cissie to be sure to bring Jane. Mrs. Thurman went upstairs to look for a suitable box.

Jane had never seen a cardboard streetcar, but she did not tell Cissie. She knew from experience that if you keep your eyes open and your wits about you, you can often save yourself from embarrassment. She would not have minded telling some people she didn't know what a streetcar parade was. But Cissie liked to show off. She liked to make you feel inferior. Of course, though, she was really a nice girl and you could have fun, once you got used to her ways.

"I couldn't find a shoe box, but I think a hat box will be even better." Mrs. Thurman returned with a large square box of glossy gray cardboard. "I put several sheets of pink and green tissue paper inside, Jane. You may wish to trade colors, or to give some to the other girls. And here are two candles. The box is so big that one would hardly make a bright enough light."

Jane could see that Cissie was envious because the box was so big. It would certainly be fun to have tissue paper to give away. Jane was always wishing she could give people things, but she almost never had anything to give. "You'd better take this knife too, as well as the scissors," Mrs. Thurman advised. "Cardboard is hard to cut."

The penknife so resembled the pearl-handled one that belonged to the nice man on the train that Jane felt suddenly buoyant. She could learn how to make a streetcar almost as good as anybody's. She would keep her wits about her and learn from watching the others. And it really was kind of Cissie to invite her.

When the two hurried up the back path, the Andrews girls and Louise had already arrived. Mrs. Matthews said they might use the dining room if they would pick up the scraps and not get paste on the furniture. It was too windy outdoors; the wind kept blowing the tissue paper away. Louise had already begun her streetcar, and while the others were discussing plans, Jane studied it to see what she was supposed to do with her own box. Along one side of Louise's box little openings of various shapes had been cut, like fancy windows. Of course! Jane realized in a flash that you pasted tissue paper over the windows and let the candle shine through like a lighted streetcar.

By the time the windows had been cut and pasted, and the long cords attached to draw the streetcars along the sidewalk, it was almost suppertime. Florence had made her windows all of pale blue, but the other girls shared their paper and had almost as many colors as a rainbow. They set the boxes in a row on the table to admire them. While Jane was admiring the clever little door, covered with yellow paper, which Alice had cut in front, she had a sudden happy idea. "Let's put passengers inside!"

"They wouldn't show from the outside," objected Cissie.

"Yes, don't you see, Cissie? We can cut little figures and color them black and paste them against the windows," explained Jane. "They'll look just like people out for a ride."

Florence and Alice were sure that nobody else would have thought of such an excellent idea. They all promised each other to keep it secret until the evening.

Richie drove them in Mrs. Thurman's surrey to Emily Welch's house. Some twenty or more streetcars and their owners had collected on Emily's front lawn. While they waited for it to grow darker, the girls examined each other's handiwork, praised it, and compared notes. A few boxes were quite elaborate, two or three stories high, with windows almost as smooth as if they had been made by machinery.

One side of India Maud's streetcar displayed a double row of windows, a trifle crooked it must be admitted, and the other side only blank cardboard. "Don't look at the other side," she begged everybody in mock dismay. "I'll be so ashamed if you do!" Then, as everyone crowded to see the blank side, she admitted cheerfully, "Well, I always was better at starting things than finishing them. Anyhow, when the parade starts I'll keep the right side toward the street and nobody who's not in on the secret will ever know."

When it was time to light the candles and begin the parade, she and Jane set their cars one behind the other. The parade was such a pretty sight that the girls took turns, two or three at a time, standing on the curbstone to watch it go by. Various little sisters and brothers and even a father or two acted as substitutes to draw the cars. The block where Emily lived had a new cement sidewalk, as smooth and level as a floor, far superior to an ordinary brick walk.

India Maud and Jane and Emily took their turn together. "It makes me wish I could be little again and believe in fairies," said Emily. "Can't you imagine how fairies would love it?"

"I never believed in them," said India Maud bluntly. "Nor

in Santa Claus either. I always liked real things better."

"Did you believe in fairies, Jane?" Emily wanted to know.

Jane shook her head somewhat regretfully. "Not really, but I used to pretend to myself I did. I always wanted to. Sometimes I made little houses for them in the apple tree."

For a few minutes they watched in silence as the little festival procession drew past them, faint lights twinkling, pools of shallow golden candleshine afloat on the deepening darkness.

"I suppose this is the last year I'll be in the parade." There was a trace of wistfulness in Emily's words. "I'm getting too old for it, and Ruthie and Martha want to have my place."

"One of them can have my place," India Maud volunteered. "I'm already too old for it and the only reason I stayed in this year was because the rest of you were and I didn't want to be left out."

Jane thought to herself that if she lived to be a hundred she would never be too old for it. It felt like the kind of good time you read about in some of the grown-up library books—with duchesses and princesses and lords strolling in illuminated gardens under the stars, and sweet music sounding from the castle, and young Sir Malcolm waiting at the garden gate for the fair Lady Beatrice. And it would so soon be ended—not only the streetcar parade, but the visits at Emily's house and Cissie's, and living with Mrs. Thurman as if she belonged.

"Don't forget tomorrow," India Maud whispered in her

ear. "Come as early as you can. Nora's going to make something extra special; don't eat much breakfast."

It was almost with apprehension that Jane rang the doorbell of the Meadows house the next noon. She need not have worried, however, for India Maud came rushing to answer it (Jane could hear her steps pounding down the hallway), and took her upstairs. She showed Jane her own room and the new den her father had furnished for himself. Then Nora rang the bell for dinner, and almost before Jane knew it she was seated at the table next to India Maud.

Mr. Meadows had come home for dinner, though he didn't usually because he didn't usually have time. He was very jolly and made jokes and teased India Maud about wearing one black shoe and one brown one to Sunday School the week before. India Maud did not mind being teased a bit. He piled Jane's plate with scalloped potatoes and fried chicken and tiny green butter beans, and told her to eat it all and come back for more, because there was plenty more where that came from. India Maud reached over and put a second spoonful of blackberry jelly on Jane's bread and butter plate, because Jane had taken so little.

Mrs. Meadows was very polite, although she did not talk much. She leaned her head on her hand as if she had a pain. Mr. Meadows asked if her head still ached. He said he would ask Dr. Ferguson to drop in, but Mrs. Meadows said no, the doctor never helped her, she would just endure it. Her voice sounded fretful. Jane noticed how white and long her fingers were and how many rings she had on. She supposed they must be real jewels, since Mr. Meadows was a banker.

Nora had made blancmange for dessert, shaped like apples, with green candy stems. Jane was pleased to find out what blancmange was, for people in books sometimes ate it. She enjoyed it, but she thought floating island had a better taste. She must tell Aggie about blancmange.

Mr. Meadows said he must be getting back to work and they must hurry if they wanted him to help hitch Daisy. "We're going now, Angeline," he told his wife as they got up from the table.

She extended a limp hand to Jane. "Come again to see India Maud some day," she said in her fretful voice.

"Of course she will!" Mr. Meadows' voice was loud and jolly as he looked over Jane's head at his wife. "We'd like to have her come every day, wouldn't we, India Maud?"

"Thank you, ma'am. Thank you, Mr. Meadows. I've had a very nice time. I hope you let India Maud come to see me at Mrs. Thurman's."

Mr. Meadows rode with them in the pony cart as far as the bank. Jane couldn't help laughing at the way he pulled his knees up. He said he was trying to make people think he was a little boy. He showed Jane how to hold the lines and let her drive all the way. She felt very gay and excited. She liked Mr. Meadows, he was so kind and jolly. If she had a father, she'd want him to be exactly like Mr. Meadows.

Before he went into the bank he told them to treat themselves. Jane saw that it was a whole quarter he gave India Maud. Even India Maud was somewhat fluttered by the size of the gift. They stopped at the candy store for five cents' worth of salted peanuts and a ten-cent paper bag of cone-shaped chocolate creams. They saved a dime for soda waters, to have later when they got thirsty.

They drove almost all afternoon, Jane holding the lines except when they had to cross the interurban tracks. She told India Maud about little Peter and how excited he got when he saw a horse, and about the invitation to Cherry Valley and how disappointed she had been because Mrs. Scott's letter had not come first.

"You're not disappointed now, are you, Jane?" India Maud asked anxiously. "You're glad you came to Danbury instead, aren't you?"

Jane let the reins fall into her lap and turned to face India Maud. "If I hadn't come to Danbury I wouldn't have had you for my best friend," she said soberly. "And I never in my whole life wanted anybody for my best friend as much as you, India Maud."

"I'm glad you feel that way, Jane, because I—" The sentence was never finished. Perverse, wily, self-willed Daisy had taken advantage of the slackened reins to stop stock-still in the middle of the streetcar tracks. No amount of slapping the lines against her plump back, no coaxing, no urging could induce her to budge. India Maud had to climb out and pull her by the bridle. Fortunately no streetcar was coming. Once she had been pulled and jerked into motion again, Daisy jogged along most amiably, only flicking her ears now and then and tossing her head to remind the girls that she had a mind of her own.

India Maud pointed out houses where girls lived who had been at Jane's party, especially Mary Bryden's because she had invited them to her house tomorrow. She showed Jane the very window in the schoolhouse beside which she sat, and the corner of the playground where the girls of the upper grades played ball. India Maud was first batter. "Oh, Jane, if only Mrs. Thurman would keep you so we could go to school together! Miss Campbell's to be our teacher and she's just wonderful. She always lets her class go nutting one Saturday and have a hay-wagon ride, with a bonfire to roast wienies and marshmallows. And when the waterworks pond freezes, everybody goes skating. You must stay in Danbury, Jane! If Angeline wasn't so nervous, you could stay at my house."

So fair was the vision painted by India Maud's words, so urgent Jane's longing to belong to that bright, inaccessible world that she had to grip the lines until her fingers hurt, to keep from forgetting herself. "Maybe Mrs. Thurman'll invite me again some time." She tried to sound lively, as if she were not giving much thought to what India Maud said.

"I wouldn't half mind speaking to her myself," India Maud pursued the subject, "or maybe George would hint to her."

Jane was shocked at the idea. "Promise me you won't," she begged. "Promise you won't even hint."

India Maud promised.

Faster and faster the days slipped by. Jane wished she could slow the time. She helped Aggie to wash dishes. She dusted her own room and the back parlor, and Aggie said she couldn't do better herself. She went with Abner to fetch cream and eggs. She helped Mrs. Thurman to pull weeds out of the flower beds, and sometimes they crocheted together on the side porch. She was making a shell-stitch shoulder shawl for Miss Fink out of some balls of lavender yarn that Mrs. Thurman said were just going to waste.

One afternoon the postman brought Jane a letter. Her heart skipped a beat and she felt shaky. What if Matron was writing her to come back? She still had almost a week left, but Matron might have forgotten. Or maybe she needed Jane. There was always a lot of work to do at the orphanage.

"Aren't you going to open your letter?" Mrs. Thurman asked.

"Yes, ma'am, I mean yes, Mrs. Thurman," answered Jane, pulling herself together. She inserted the steel crochet hook in the flap of the envelope and slit it open. The letter was a single page. "Matron says Mrs. Scott wants me to come to Cherry Valley after all, and her niece is going to stay all next month." Jane was jubilant. "She's sent a ticket and I'm to go straight from Danbury."

"You wish to go so much?"

"I never wanted anything so much in my whole life. And that was before I even knew how wonderful it is to live in a real house like other people. Matron says I can finish out my two visits." Jane drew a deep, ecstatic breath. "Mrs. Scott's niece is just about my age. Her name's Letitia."

"Do you always visit in two places?"

For a moment Jane thought Mrs. Thurman must be joking. "Didn't Matron tell you this is the first time I ever visited? The very first!"

Mrs. Thurman laid down her knitting. "Is it very different from the Home?"

Eager though Jane was to have her understand the difference, she must not let her think she was unhappy at the Home, because she wasn't. It was hard to choose words to tell both sides at once. "Oh, we're very well taken care of, Mrs. Thurman. We have plenty to eat and good clothes to wear and we don't have to work any more than is good for children of our age. Matron is very kind and so is Miss Fink. They both look after us as if they were our own mothers—I mean about taking care of us if we get sick and seeing that we take care of our clothes and learn good manners and how to behave. But of course it's not the same as a real family in a house.

"There's a board fence, and we can't see over. I don't think people ought to be shut up behind board fences, even for their own good, do you?" She paused, remembering how privileged and cheerful it felt to unlatch the gate here and walk through.

Mrs. Thurman was looking across the shady stretch of grass to the opening in the bridal wreath hedge, where the path led down to the road and the road led away to the open country.

"The thing I mind the most, the thing almost everybody minds most, isn't being shut in—because of course we have a good big playground, covered with cinders so we can play even when it rains. The worst thing is not having anybody belonging to you. At school when the others talk about their houses and their families and their dogs and all their other things, you can't help feeling left out."

"Did you wish to visit in Danbury too, Jane?" Mrs. Thurman inquired after a time.

Jane tried to explain without hurting her feelings. "You see I wasn't sure you'd really want me. You might think you had to take me anyhow."

"Now that we're acquainted, you must come again, Jane

girl."

Deep within her mind Jane heard the words like bells echoing and re-echoing from room to far room. They had a belonging sound, like notes sung in tune. "I mustn't do all the visiting," she said eagerly. "You must visit me, Mrs. Thurman. When I'm grown I'm going to have a house."

Rover, who never liked to be left out, poked his nose into Jane's lap. She squeezed him hard and scratched his head. "Of course you're invited too," she assured him. "I'll save the bones specially."

When India Maud and Emily drove over in the pony cart later in the afternoon, Mrs. Thurman suggested that they make fudge. Although Jane had never made it, she knew enough about it not to be uneasy. India Maud declared that the whole secret of fudge is to set it in cold water to cool. Emily was quite positive that the secret is never to stir it while it is cooking.

Aggie, who was setting out the sugar and cream and chocolate and butter, had to arbitrate. "Draw straws and settle the argument." She pulled two straws from the top of the kitchen broom. "Long wins. You get your way this time, Em'ly."

Emily was willing to yield a point, however, and let the others take turns at stirring, especially as her practiced nose detected a faint odor of scorching cream and sugar. The fudge smelled so delicious, bubbling thickly as it cooked, and the

trial spoonfuls dropped into a cup of cold water at frequent intervals were so tantalizing that they could hardly wait. The moment they set the pan in cold water they began to beat, and the candy was still hot when they poured it out into the buttered cake pan. While they waited for it to harden, they scooped along the edges with spoons and ate. Abner said it was "a hull mile better'n store-bought candy." They'd make better cooks than Aggie if only they'd keep in practice.

As they washed the pans and straightened the kitchen they chattered like sparrows. India Maud intended to organize a club. She had thought of a wonderful name, a Latin name. Only the members would know what the name meant. Well, she hadn't really thought up the name all by herself. Her cousin was studying Latin in high school and he had helped.

Jane tried to keep her mind on something else. It would not do to keep remembering that she would be back at the Home when school began. Now and then she joined in the conversation. Not for worlds would she have let India Maud and Emily suspect that she felt left out. They did not mean to leave her out, she knew; they just forgot.

A shadow darkened the last days of Jane's visit. In the middle of supper or while she was getting ready for bed with a book propped open on the bird's-eye maple dressing table, she would think "Only four days more" —or three, or two. Sometimes, while she dried the plates for Aggie, she would imagine

Aggie at the sink washing dishes alone, and a catch would come in her breath. Then she would clear her throat and talk very cheerfully about something India Maud or Emily or Cissie had told her, something funny to make Aggie laugh.

Aggie and Mrs. Thurman seemed not to be aware how fast the time was melting away. Sometimes Jane wished they would notice and speak of it, so she would not feel quite so lonesome; and sometimes she was glad they did not mention it. "Don't you feel sorry for yourself, Jane Douglas! You've had a scrumptious visit and now you're going to Cherry Valley," she told herself sensibly. "There's lots of children that would be glad to have even one visit. You didn't expect it to last forever, did you, silly?"

She decided to wear the pink gingham on the train. Abner had mended the broken strap on the valise so that it looked almost as good as new, and Aggie made sandwiches of chopped sweet pickle and boiled ham, wrapped in oiled paper. Mrs. Thurman went with Jane to the station.

They sat almost like strangers on the back seat of the surrey. Jane held herself stiffly erect, not to wrinkle the freshly laundered pink dress. She felt almost as ill at ease as that first evening in the back parlor. She would have liked to converse in a grown-up, ladylike way. She would have liked to tell Mrs. Thurman what a wonderful visit it had been and how she would remember it always. Instead she sat wordless, looking at the back of Richie's head, listening to him and Mrs. Thurman laugh at old Polly's tricks to get her own way.

The brakeman set the gray canvas valise on the train. "All aboard," he called. "All abo-oard! Martinsville, Summit, Paris, Cherry Valley!"

Jane's foot was on the step. Suddenly she ducked under the surprised brakeman's arm and went racing back. "Oh, please, Mrs. Thurman, if ever I can do you a favor, please let me know. You've been so nice to me, I'd like awfully to do you a favor." She had to run to reach the train before it started. "Good-bye, ma'am."

8

CHERRY VALLEY

JANE saw Mr. Scott and Letitia before the train stopped. Mr. Scott was wearing a Panama hat and a gray seersucker suit. Letitia was tall. The top of her head reached almost to his shoulder. She was swinging a yellow straw hat from which bunches of daisies threatened momentarily to fly loose. Jane thought she had never seen such pretty brown curls as Letitia's, tied with a bow behind each ear.

The two hurried along beside the train, waving as they ran. Mr. Scott lifted Jane off the high step and set her down on the platform with a bantering, "Don't pass us by, Miss Janie!"

"Don't pay any attention to Uncle John," Letitia advised, linking her arm in Jane's. "He's an old tease."

Mr. Scott set the valise in the buggy and crowded himself in beside the girls. As soon as he lifted the reins the horses were off, nimble and brisk, as if they were showing off especially

for Jane's benefit. Jane had time only to notice that Cherry Valley was too small to be a real town—one or two stores, a church, and a string of houses scattered along under the trees.

"How do you like farming?" Mr. Scott asked, leaning forward to look past Letitia at Jane, who sat clutching the iron bar of the buggy seat with one hand and her round-crowned hat with the other. The horses were trotting so fast she was almost afraid of falling out.

"I've never been on a farm," she told him shyly. The words flew out like a ribbon in the breeze the buggy made.

"You mean to say— Well, well! We can't have any city girls here! We'll soon make a country girl of you, young lady." The threatening tone did not dampen Jane's pleasure; in fact it increased it, for she could hear the laugh underneath the gruffness. Besides, she had caught the twinkle in his eyes. India Maud's father sometimes joked like that too, pretending to be stern and cross when he was really only teasing.

Mr. Scott gave the team its head, now that they were out of the village. "A week ago Tish was just as citified as you, Janie, but now we can't tell which is Tish and which is cornstalks. Her Aunt Callie rings the dinner bell, and if the stalk stands still it's corn. If it comes running for biscuits and honey, its Tish." He shot a sidelong glance at the two girls to see how they took the joke.

"Isn't he just *awful?*" Letitia pretended to be shocked. "The whoppers he tells!"

Jane laughed out loud. In imagination she could see the cornstalks flapping their long green arms and trying clumsily to lift their rooted feet. She would have liked to make a joke herself about the poor hungry cornstalks, but she guessed she didn't know the Scotts well enough yet. They might think she was too forward. "Your uncle likes to tease you, doesn't he, Letitia?" she commented sedately.

"Don't you think I'm positively angelic to let him?" Tish leaned back with a smile. "But call me Tish, Jane; all my friends do. I'm trying to think of a nickname for you."

Jane wished she were two persons, one to talk and listen, and one to watch the country as they sped by. There were fields of wheat bending like golden waves under the light summer wind, and cornfields like endless tents of green with brown earth showing between the long, straight rows. There were shady woodland clumps, and a river which ran out from the woods to slide under a red wooden bridge that rattled noisily as they rode over. "Is it far to your farm, Mr. Scott?" She just couldn't wait any longer to ask that question.

"Mr. Scott?" He frowned. "Who in all-get-out is he? I'm Uncle John, but I don't see any second gentleman by the name of Scott."

"Uncle John, I mean," she corrected herself shyly.

"That's better." His face cleared. "How far to the farm?

It's exactly two and three-eighths miles from the railroad depot to our front door. Now shut your eyes" (Jane screwed them tight) "and open them when I say—scat!"

Jane saw a clump of trees shading a white house, and beyond it a great red barn and several smaller ones, red and brown and gray. She kept her eyes on the house, watching it grow in size as they approached. It was much smaller than the barn and only part of it was two stories high, but anybody could see that nice people lived there.

Mrs. Scott hurried out to greet them, an apron over her head to keep the sun from her eyes, but she whisked it off and extended both hands to help Jane from the buggy. "I hope the train ride hasn't tired you, Janie."

"Not the least bit, Mrs. Scott," Jane assured her politely. She knew that Mrs. Scott had asked just to be polite, because of course nobody ever got tired from riding on the train.

"There she goes, Scotting us again," growled Uncle John, following them across the yard with the valise. "Jane, this is your Aunt Callie. The family Bible says *Caroline,* but I don't believe it, even if it's in the Bible. The only time anybody ever called her that was when the minister pronounced us man and wife. I thought he was marrying me to the wrong person."

"Isn't he dreadful!" Tish looked at Jane to make sure she appreciated his joking.

"Take Jane to the back porch to wash her hands. Supper's

on the table. Jack and Reuben want to get an early start to call on their girls." Mrs. Scott hurried into the kitchen. She said she was having to look after things all by herself, since Molly was spending a few days with her father. Jane wondered who Molly was, but she supposed she'd find out by and by.

While Jane washed her hands and face and dried them on the long roller towel that hung against the porch wall, she and Tish got better acquainted. They had liked each other at first sight. "You can't think how exciting it is to be on a farm," she confided to Tish. "It's like having all my wishes come true, all at once."

"I hope you brought some overalls." Tish's manner promised better things to come, but Jane thought nothing could make her happier than she was at that very moment. "Dresses are no good to climb trees and help plow. Never mind," as Jane shook her head, "Aunt Callie'll fix you up. Do you like to ride horseback?"

Jane straightened the portion of the towel she had been using. She was pleased to see that she had not left any black marks. "I've honestly never been on a horse." She hoped Tish would not think less of her when she learned how few adventurous experiences she had had.

"I'm not so very good on a horse myself," Tish confessed candidly, "but you ought to hear me brag when I get home.

I tell them I'm as good as a circus rider. They don't believe me, except maybe Grandma, but it's fun to brag anyhow."

When Jane looked up from the table after the blessing, she was facing two young men. "Jane—Jack and Reuben," their father introduced them.

Jane nodded politely, and they nodded back. "Pleased to meet you," she said in a low voice, and "The same to you," they answered in one breath.

Jane was glad she wasn't in such a hurry as they were. Although she was quite as famished as Tish announced herself to be, the supper was too good to swallow in a hurry. From time to time as she glanced up from her plate of mashed potatoes and chicken gravy, of sweet corn fried in butter, of fried chicken and homemade cucumber pickle, she was conscious of Jack's and Reuben's eyes. She could see that they were not watching her, though. They only wanted to get used to her, to know what she was like. She liked their looks; they looked friendly. They were sunburned and their eyes were brown and so was their hair. They had on clean white shirts with the collars turned back for coolness.

"What about honey on your biscuit, Jane?" Uncle John passed a glass bowl with a comb of honey inside and a curved spoon made of bone. "Too bad your friend Tish doesn't like it!"

"Don't believe a word he says, Jane. If I could choose just

one thing to eat all the rest of my life," Tish declared, "it would be biscuits and butter and honey."

"That's three things," Jane reminded her with a little giggle, helping herself to the honey.

Tish giggled too. "I'm no good at arithmetic. I can't even count. Papa tells me so every time he has to help with my homework."

Jane had never tasted hot biscuits and honey. The first taste convinced her that nothing, not even peach ice cream and devil's food cake, was so good. The biscuits were small, light tan on top and bottom, and snowy white when you split them open to spread the butter. They were so hot that you had to rest them on your plate, and the butter melted in tiny golden pools and ran down the sides unless you were quick and careful. On top of the butter you put the honey, and before it began to drip over the edge you bit in the most likely place. It was clover honey, Aunt Callie said, from their own hives. It tasted the way a field of clover blossoms smelled, only much better because of the buttery hot biscuit.

Tish and Jane slept in a bed wide enough for a whole family. It was a feather bed, high, thick, and puffy. At first they kept rolling into each other in the middle of the bed, but after a while they got sleepy and made themselves each a private hollow.

In the morning they lay in bed and talked. Jane thought

perhaps they ought to help with the breakfast. Tish stretched lazily and said no, Aunt Callie wanted her to get her sleep out every morning, and she could have her breakfast whenever she wanted it. Suddenly, however, she bounced bolt upright, sniffing the air like a puppy.

"Pancakes!" She slid quickly out of bed. "We'll have to hurry. Aunt Callie won't bake them just for me."

They dressed hastily and washed their hands and faces in the round china bowl on the walnut washstand. It required four hands to lift the big, blue and white water pitcher.

"Smelled the cakes, did you?" Uncle John greeted them. "I told Callie she'd better count on a few extras. Tish can smell pancakes a mile off." He tweaked her knot of curls.

"Set plates for yourselves." Aunt Callie lifted the other leaf of the kitchen table. "We breakfast out here to save steps," she explained to Jane, " 'specially when I'm frying cakes and Molly's not here to help."

The boys had had breakfast and gone to the neighbor's, where the combine was threshing. Uncle John said the combine was due to come to him on Monday. The prospect of threshers made Tish rejoice.

"I missed it last year," she told Jane. "You never saw so much to eat, and some of the wives come to help out, and of course ever so many men. We can carry water to the men in the field, and help wait on table. It's better than a Sunday

School picnic, isn't it, Aunt Callie?"

Aunt Callie was noncommittal about the resemblance be-tween a picnic and threshing, but she hoped they would have plenty to eat. "Which reminds me," addressing her husband, "do you think the two girls could drive Whitey to the Valley? I'm short of baking powder, and they might as well bring back a fifty-pound bag of sugar and some rubber rings for canning while they're about it."

Uncle John laughed. "Whitey knows the way there and back. Why don't you just put a note in the whip socket? Oh, I suppose it won't do any harm for Tishie and Janie to go along," he added teasingly. "Company for old Whitey, you might say."

Tish was on the point of pummeling him, but the ringing of what sounded like sleigh bells announced an arrival. The girls rushed out to see. It was the huckster wagon, drawn by a pair of sleek, sad-eyed mules. Jane had never seen anything like it. There were rows of narrow shelves built one above the other on the outside of the wagon, just like a store, with an aisle down the middle, and a latched gate at the back. On the high seat, under a huge cotton umbrella that shaded the front half of the wagon, perched a bright-eyed old man with a long beard.

" 'Day, Miz' Scott. 'Day, John." He nodded genially. "Good thrashin' weather, I call it. When's the combine comin' to you, John?"

While their elders discussed weather, crops, and news, the two girls ranged up and down both sides of the wagon, alert as robins spying out a new berrybush. The shelves were crowded with an amazing array—almost everything imaginable, and all very useful, as Jane pointed out to Tish in an undertone. On the lowest shelves were pans and lids and kettles, held in place by a thin wooden bar. "He puts them on the bottom because if they get dusty all anybody has to do is wash them," explained Tish. There were brooms and baskets, coils of rope and binding-twine, a floor mop, dusty steel knives and forks and enameled wash basins and tin plates, bunches of cotton gloves, a faded baseball mitt and a bag of marbles.

"I can't think of a single thing he hasn't got," Jane whispered as they detected two half-bolts of blue calico wrapped in yellowed newspaper.

Uncle John fetched a pail of eggs from the icebox for Aunt Callie, who passed it on to the huckster. "There's five dozen," she told him.

"Eggs ain't fetchin' much." He spoke much less cheerfully than when he had talked of the hot weather. Jane thought he didn't want Aunt Callie to get her hopes too high. "Everybody's got all the eggs they need. But yours is such good ones, Miz' Scott, that I'm willin' to give a mite extry. How say to sixteen and a half cents? That's a whole half cent a dozen more than I been givin'. Can't get much more'n that for 'em myself when I sell 'em to the store."

Mrs. Scott said she'd have to take what she could get, but it hardly paid to sell. She'd take the money out in trade. Did he have any rubber rings for Mason jars? No, he'd sold the last to Miz' Stepney. If she was taking the eggs out in trade though, he could pay a mite more—say eighteen cents a dozen. Aunt Callie seemed pleased to have a better bargain. She could use an extra stewpan, with threshers coming.

After she had selected a pan and Mr. Abraham had dusted it off and handed it back to her, together with seventeen cents in change, he reached behind him and pulled out a drawer. He fumbled in the drawer and extracted the lid of a shoe box piled with candy. "Here." He extended the lid toward Jane and Tish. "You young'uns can have a treat." When they hesitated out of politeness, he insisted. "Choose for yourselves," he said with a generous gesture. "One apiece. It's a free present I'm makin' you."

There were so many kinds of candy jumbled together that it was difficult to make a choice. Tish selected a whip of black licorice and Jane a pink banana made of something resembling marshmallow, but much tougher and flavored with cinnamon.

They watched the wagon go swaying down the lane, the red cotton umbrella fluttering in the morning breeze, the loose cargo rattling pleasantly. "You know what?" Jane remarked as she offered Tish a bite of pink banana, "if we had a wagon like that we could put beds inside and live in it all summer. We could pay our way out of the profits."

Tish's reply was more or less inarticulate, the banana so filled her mouth, but she seemed to approve the suggestion.

"We'll let Whitey walk until we get out of sight," she said to Jane when they started to the Valley. "Then we'll make her trot. I wish Uncle John had given us a buggy whip."

Whitey had no intention of bestirring herself on so warm a day. In vain the girls pulled and sawed at the lines, in vain they let them lie slack, gee'd and hawed and wheedled and scolded. Whitey's speckled white flanks heaved up and down at the same slow, deliberate gait.

"Let's give up hurrying and enjoy ourselves," suggested Jane. "It's fun to be out riding."

It was a relief to give up the struggle with Whitey. "There's where we're coming to the sociable tomorrow." Tish indicated the white church at the edge of the village. "Aunt Callie always takes ice cream. I hope she makes an extra amount for us."

"Does the sociable cost much?" Jane thought of her two nickels and the dollar bill Matron had given her. She doubted whether Matron would consider a sociable an emergency.

"No." Tish was indifferent. "Nothing costs much in the country."

When they reached the Al. S. Peters General Store. Mdse. and Groceries, Whitey stopped of her own accord. Jane held the lines while Tish went into the store. She came out carrying the jar rings and baking powder can, followed by Al Peters lugging a big cloth bag of sugar. He dropped it into the buggy and then stepped back to survey the two girls.

"Want I should turn her around?" he offered. "You don't look like old hands at drivin'."

"No, thank you." Tish's pride had been touched. "I know how to turn around." She flapped the lines smartly against Whitey's fat back and pulled toward the left.

Without moving the shaft, Whitey gave a half-hearted, partial turn of her head. Jane helped Tish pull on the left line. Whitey lifted one heavy forefoot, held it a few inches above the ground, then set it down in precisely the same spot. Tish tugged manfully, her cheeks very red and her mouth in a straight line. Al Peters laughed. Jane wanted to laugh too, for Whitey's expression, as she rolled her eye back at them with her head drooped pathetically over the shaft, reminded her of little Peter. When Peter tried to get his own way he looked at you with exactly the same hurt, pitiful expression. Jane did not laugh though. She could see that Tish did not think it was funny.

"Why wouldn't it be a good idea to drive straight ahead and around the block?" Jane was careful to keep her voice soft so that Al Peters could not hear.

Tish made no answer, but she loosened the left line and slapped Whitey vigorously across the back. Reluctantly, Whitey pulled her head over the shaft and faced forward. Encouraged, Tish whacked her again. Gradually Whitey began to move and the wheels to turn. Tish wisely decided to let her take her own time.

Neither girl said anything until they were well on the way. Then Tish muttered, half under her breath, "What made me maddest wasn't Whitey. It was that Al Peters. He'll tell Uncle John and make it sound lots worse and we'll never hear the last of it."

Jane noticed that Tish was frowning less and that her cheeks were not so red. She ventured to joke a little. "Honestly, Tish, it's so much fun to hear Uncle John tease you that I hope Al Peters does tell. And I like the way you get back at Uncle John. Some people get mad, but you know just how to take it."

Something resembling a smile flickered across Tish's hot face. "Oh, I can get even with Uncle John when he teases. And," she admitted, relaxing a little, "I suppose it was funny."

Cheered by the sight of the home pasture, Whitey pricked up her ears and quickened her plodding gait to a steady trot Their dashing entrance to the barn lot drew a long whistle of admiration from Enoch, the hired man who was forking down hay.

9

THE CHURCH SOCIABLE

UNCLE JOHN was going to drive to the schoolhouse. A window had been reported broken, and since he lived nearer than the other members of the School Board, it was his duty to keep an eye on the school. Would the girls like to go?

It was a one-room, country schoolhouse, with pegs for hanging hats and coats, and in the center of the room an iron stove. Somebody had recently made a fire, Uncle John said, and cooked a meal. He slammed the stove door shut upon blackened cobs of roasting ears and scorched chicken feathers and bones. Gypsies; no doubt of it, he said. They had a great way of breaking into schoolhouses. A trashy, thieving tribe, who'd liefer rob an honest man's corn patch and hen roost than do a day's work. Well, he'd have to get a pane of glass from the Valley and putty in the window. The girls could go with him or wait here.

They chose to wait. It was fun to write on the blackboard, and dust the erasers, and lift the lids of the desks to look inside, although except for an occasional pencil stub or scrap of paper they proved disappointingly empty. Even the teacher's desk contained nothing, not even a pitch-pipe or a pointer to use when they took turns pretending to be the teacher.

Tish was beginning to be bored. "I'm going to see what's in the cellar. I'll bet there's something besides stove wood."

Though neither would have admitted it, they were both a bit nervous as they felt their way cautiously down the crude steps. Having started upon the venture, however, neither was willing to be the first to turn back. At the foot of the steps they stood close together, trying to see in the semi-darkness. As their eyes grew accustomed to the gloom, they made out something white—a figure stretched on a table, dimly outlined under a sheet. Tish clutched at Jane; and Jane, for her part, had to stiffen her knees to keep from yielding to her own and Tish's fear.

Without a word, silent as shadows, they turned and groped their way on tiptoe up the stairs. The sound of their own breathing was loud in their ears, and their dresses, as they brushed against the stair wall, sighed like ghosts. At the head of the stairs Tish made a dash for the open front door, but Jane stopped. Her feet, her legs, her whole body wanted to escape with Tish, but her inner self—the same self that so often vexed her with doubts and worries—would not let her go until she had carefully closed the cellar door and slid the heavy bolt into place.

They sat on the stile in the hot sun and waited for Uncle John. "It must be somebody the gypsies left there." Tish was still afraid to speak above a whisper though the wind was loud in the hickory trees and the sun shone bright in their faces. "What if it tries to come after us?" She shivered.

"It can't," Jane stated flatly. "I locked the door."

Silence followed. They watched the empty road with anxious eyes. The minutes lengthened, the wind made little brown whorls and spirals in the road dust, and still there was no sign of a horse and buggy.

"Anyhow, it wasn't the gypsies that left it there," Jane broke the heavy silence.

"How do you know? I'm positive it was gypsies," stated Tish.

"Because I have a gypsy friend. They don't do things like that." Jane's quiet statement admitted no argument. "Maybe sometimes they take things to eat that don't belong to them, but that's all."

When at last Uncle John arrived, Tish threw herself upon him with such a breathless flood of words that he had to ask Jane what she was trying to tell him. "She says there's a dead man in the cellar." Jane's voice was not quite steady.

With a muttered ejaculation he shoved Tish aside and strode into the building. At the sight of his serious face the girls' half-forgotten alarm revived, and they clung to each other. Tish was in tears.

A minute or two later he was back, mopping his hot face between bursts of laughter. "Almost scared me out of a year's growth, you two! Come with me; I've something to show you." He took them both by the shoulder and marched them into the school and down the cellar steps. "Now take a good look!" He lifted the covering from the sheeted figure.

Stacks of old school books, a tall vase or two, and a geography globe lay revealed. Jane giggled, and after a moment Tish joined her. "It's a good thing I didn't go for the sheriff," said Jane.

After they were back at the farm, the two sat in the shade of the horse-chestnut tree, resting from their adventure and refreshing themselves with ice cream. Aunt Callie had just taken the dasher out of the freezer and given it to them to scrape. "I'm glad it wasn't Molly that took the dasher out," said Tish, drawing her spoon accurately along the under side of a blade. "She'd have scraped all the ice cream back into the freezer."

Now was Jane's chance to inquire about Molly.

"She helps Aunt Callie. She's like a hired girl, only she's

not really, because she's a kind of cousin. It gives her extra pin money to spend." Tish giggled as a blob of ice cream melted and dropped on her chin. "Only Molly never spends. She puts it all in the bank. Uncle John says she must have quite a tidy sum laid by."

"Maybe she has to save." Jane knew what it was to have no money to spend.

"She could spend if she wanted to. She's got something in mind to do with it," Tish hinted darkly.

Jane asked what.

But Tish had to admit that she didn't know. "Reuben thinks he knows, but I can't make him tell me. I'm just dying to find out."

"Is she your cousin too?" Jane was interested in Molly.

"I 'spose so. Her mother married a man that Grandpa strictly commanded her not to. Reuben says their place is going to rack and ruin."

Jane felt sorry for Molly, but she did not think Tish would understand.

"Some day we'll go see Aunt Lidy Spence," said Tish, changing the subject. "Her parlor's crammed with interesting things like sea shells and pink and white coral branches. She's got a talking-machine too, and a music box, and she lets you play them as much as you want to. We'll plan to go on a day when Molly can't go with us. That Molly!" Tish frowned and attempted a disdainful whistle, but the sound that came from her lips was only a feeble wheeze, scarcely louder than the rustle of a leaf. "Molly says don't get dirt on the carpet and don't handle anything, you might break it, and don't stay too long, you might wear your welcome out." She mimicked Molly's brusque manner.

"Better bring that dasher here," a voice called from the kitchen door. "I can't keep the dishwater waiting all day." The screen door banged shut.

"That's Molly. She must have come back while we were at the schoolhouse." Tish looked somewhat uneasy. She was probably afraid Molly might have heard what she said about her, Jane thought. "Did you notice her red hair?" Tish had recovered from her momentary alarm. "You know what red hair's a sign of, don't you?" Tish caught at Jane's skirt to help pull herself off the ground.

Later that day, Jane asked Uncle John if two nickels were enough for the sociable. But he told her to put her money away; ladies were not allowed to pay, and he was going to buy a family ticket. Jane was glad she did not have to break Matron's dollar.

They went in the spring wagon. The rubber-tired carriage was new and Aunt Callie would not have it scratched and stained by the ice-cream freezer. Tish and Jane sat with Uncle John on the high seat in front, and Aunt Callie and Molly on the second seat, each with a cake covered with a clean dish-towel balanced on her lap. The freezer sat on the wagon bed, with an old piece of carpet underneath to keep it from sliding when the wagon jolted.

It was still daylight when they reached the church, but the crowd was already beginning to gather—mostly ladies with their husbands and cakes and freezers of ice cream. There were several children, but Tish was not acquainted with them.

Boards had been laid over sawhorses to make a long table, and wires strung from tree to tree for gay-colored Chinese lanterns with candles inside, ready to light as soon as it grew dark. Two or three men were busy unscrewing the carriage lamps from their buggies to fasten to trees where they would shine on the table. The ladies would need a bright light to serve the refreshments. They were spreading tablecloths over the boards and arranging vases of marigolds and cosmos.

Jane and Tish and two sisters named Ivy and Pearl set plates and spoons along the edge of the table. The spoons belonged to the Ladies' Aid. The plates were of thin wood, fluted at the rim. Ivy said she was surely glad there wouldn't be plates to wash, because she and Pearl always had to help. They got more dishwashing at home than you could shake a stick at. There were eight children in their family and they were all boys except them. The boys never had to help with the dishes.

Now that it was growing dusk, the men lighted the Chinese

lanterns and the ladies began to uncover the cakes and remove the tops from the freezers. The first customers were boys, a jostling, good-natured crowd of them, from quite little fellows to some as big as Jack and Reuben.

"Come on." Ivy spoke with the voice of authority. "Let's watch the cakes being cut and see which looks best. Some of the Ladies' Aid're awful poor cake-makers. Be sure not to get Mis' Featherson's ice cream. It's full of cornstarch lumps. She let us sample it because we helped get her things out of the buggy. That's her in the blue apron with ruffles."

As the four girls wandered up and down the long table, studying the cakes to see which had the most layers and thickest icing, and watching the ice cream turned out of the cone-shaped scoops to see who gave the biggest servings, other girls joined them. Conversation was fragmentary, carried on in undertones and whispers.

"Ask Jed Jones if that caramel cake's as good as it looks," urged one. "Ask him yourself," giggled another. "He's in your class at school."

"Look what stingy pieces Mis' Featherson is cutting out of her chocolate cake." Ivy was indignant. "I'll bet she's trying to save half to take home."

Jane felt proud to see the thick slices Aunt Callie cut from her cocoanut layer-cakes. And Molly, beside her, dishing out ice cream, was giving big helpings too. Jane decided to choose

Aunt Callie's ice cream and cake, but not because the servings were big. She liked Aunt Callie so much that she wanted her to sell out faster than the others. Tish craved variety. Why take Aunt Callie's when you could have it anyhow?

They carried their plates of refreshments over to the row of girls sitting on the low railing which separated the church lawn from the cemetery. The boys, who had congregated behind the church, came back by two's and three's to have their plates refilled. The men gathered in small groups, leaning against the white weather-boarded walls of the church or standing in knots beside the hitching posts. They seemed to be talking about the horses, for occasionally one would lift a hoof to examine it or peer appraisingly into a horse's mouth.

Tish nudged Jane, almost making her spill her ice cream. "Look," she said. "Where do you suppose Molly's going?"

Molly had removed her apron and was walking toward the road, her long, starched white skirt sweeping the grass. A single-seated buggy was waiting, with the top folded back. Molly climbed in, the man touched the whip, and the horse started off at a brisk canter. Nobody else seemed to notice. Jane and Tish decided not to mention it. After all, Molly was a kind of cousin.

They caught sight of Jack with a girl. Jane and Tish slid off the fence and quietly maneuvered themselves into a position where they could get a good look. Jack wore his Sunday clothes

and the girl had a ruffled white dress with a black velvet bow
at the waist. Her face was turned toward Jack's, and the lan-
tern light showed her fair skin and the wavy lights in her hair.

"I know who she is," Tish whispered. "She's Grace Barry,
and she goes to college. She's in the same class with my brother
and Jack."

The two girls quietly resumed their places on the fence.
They did not wish Jack to think they were spying on him.
"I didn't know he went to college," said Jane.

"He's studying to be a scientific farmer. Grandma doesn't
believe in it; she says it's nonsense to think you can learn to
farm out of books. I want a chafing dish to make candy when
I go to college."

Jane had never thought about college. Nobody at the orphanage had ever mentioned it. "Does it cost a lot of money
to go?" she asked.

"I guess it's practically free except you have to pay for board
and room, and my brother spends a lot for fraternity pins and
things. His pin's solid gold with a real pearl. It doesn't do
him any good, though; he lets his girl wear it."

Jane longed to know what a fraternity pin was, but she did
not ask. She would wait and find out. She wondered if she
would ever go to college. Yes, she had made up her mind, this
very instant. She would find a way to earn money to pay her
way. There were always families with babies to be taken

care of.

"Yes, I'm going to college," she told Tish. It was like making a promise out loud. But Tish's attention was elsewhere.

"I hear an automobile," she said excitedly. "It must be Reuben and his girl. Her family's got one. Let's go see."

It was Reuben, at the wheel of a red horseless carriage, with a girl at his side. The man and woman on the back seat got out.

From behind the church the boys came pushing pell-mell to examine the automobile. Jane would have liked to join them, to take her turn at giving a trial twist to the steering wheel, to run her hands over the smooth shining brass and red enamel, to put one foot up on the running board and lean against the horseless carriage as if it belonged to her, the way the boys did. But of course she couldn't; it would not be ladylike. Besides, Tish did not seem to be particularly interested in the carriage.

After a little while the automobile, carrying only Reuben and the girl, started off with a loud explosive sound and a series of chugging coughs. The crowd of boys drifted away. Jane could hear their voices rise and fall, and now and then a guffaw of laughter. She couldn't help thinking it was too bad that nobody was riding in the back seat. There was plenty of room for three people, or even four, if they didn't mind being crowded a little.

"I've ridden in an auto four or five times," Tish remarked

when the two had resumed their position on the fence. "Our next door neighbor has one. It feels funny with the machinery going and no horse to pull you. Grandma says the Lord never intended folks to ride in such contraptions. She says horses are good enough for her."

After that they sat in silence, each occupied with her own thoughts. The crowd was beginning to thin out and most of the girls had rejoined their families. Behind the dark trees in the cemetery the rim of the rising moon shone bright gold. Jane wondered about the people shut up in the graves. Did they know about the ice-cream sociable, and the horseless carriage, and the rows of Chinese lanterns hanging beneath the boughs like round, flowery moons? Could they hear the ladies laughing among themselves as they began to gather up the plates and freezers? Did it make them feel happier to hear? Or were they sad because they must stay still and lonesome under the dark earth? She hoped there weren't any children in the graves.

She shook herself. "This fence is getting sharp."

"We can't sit on the grass because of chiggers," yawned Tish. "Let's sit in the wagon."

A bonfire had been built of green switches to keep mosquitoes away. The horses' eyes glowed in the firelight like live coals. It was hard to walk in the dark; the ground was rough and you kept stumbling. The broad wagon seat felt com-

fortable beneath you. Tish was so sleepy that she tried to lie down in the seat. Jane moved to the back. She was sleepy too, but there would be time enough to sleep when she was back at the Home. The shadows of the trees black against the sky, the colored lanterns glowing in the dark air, and the sounds of voices and of horses nickering and pawing made her feel excited.

She thought of Peter. Maybe when he was big enough to look after himself Uncle John and Aunt Callie would invite him to visit. She wished Miss Fink could have a piece of Aunt Callie's cake; Miss Fink almost never had good things. Matron sometimes had Cook do something special, like an apple dumpling or a blackberry roly-poly. Matron paid for it out of her own money. Miss Fink couldn't afford to pay for extras.

Aunt Callie and Uncle John were coming towards the wagon. She could see them quite plainly in the bonfire light, though it was burning low. Uncle John was carrying the freezer, and Aunt Callie's hands were filled with cake pans and dishtowels and two ice-cream scoops. Jane jumped down to help her. Tish sat up and yawned.

"Isn't Molly going home with us?" Tish inquired.

"She's got better company and a rubber-tired rig to ride in." Uncle John sounded sleepy too. "Are you going to let your Aunt Callie ride all alone back there?"

"I'll sit in the back," Jane offered. "Honestly, I want to," she insisted when Aunt Callie suggested that the front seat would be more comfortable.

The jolting of the wagon roused Tish, and Jane could hear her voice in animated conversation with Uncle John, though she could not make out the words. Aunt Callie was pleased with the way the refreshments had sold; it was the biggest turn-out of the summer. The Aid hoped to make enough money to paint the church.

"Don't you children get up for breakfast till you're a mind to," Aunt Callie called after them as they stumbled up the stairs. "It's Sunday and there's nothing to get up for." It was not the preacher's week to be at the Valley.

Tish fell asleep immediately, but Jane kept remembering things though she was not trying to remember. . . . Molly held her head high like Mrs. Thurman. Molly was prettier than anyone else at the sociable. Even if her hair was red it was pretty, with little curls getting loose from under the crown of thick braids. If you didn't know she was a hired girl you would think she was rich.

Grace Barry was pretty too. Jane had read stories about college girls and the scrapes they got into and the midnight feasts they had, with cakes hidden under the bed, and alcohol lamps to make cocoa. College must be different from school. At school you seemed to get into trouble instead of having scrapes. She was glad she did not often get into trouble.

She was pleased she had been to a sociable. Matron and Miss Fink sometimes went to one at the Baptist Church, but of course they did not take the children. It would cost too much. Things seemed to cost more in town than in the country. She wondered if Mrs. Thurman went to sociables.

She thought of Aggie in her good-smelling kitchen, and Abner with his old hat shoved back on his head, and Alice White bending over the sewing machine to stitch Jane's new dresses. Did Aggie miss her when she washed dishes, and did Rover sometimes go nosing and poking from one room to another to look for her, the way he looked for Mrs. Thurman? Would Mrs. Thurman remember that she had said she would invite Jane again next summer?

"Don't you go thinking about next summer and get your hopes too high," she warned herself soberly. "Besides, you ought to be thinking how to do Mrs. Thurman a favor instead of hoping she'll do you one."

In spite of all she could do, however, hopes kept rising to float through her thoughts like bright bubbles.

10

THE ELOPEMENT

Oh, my goodness!" Aunt Callie jumped up hastily. "The chickens are out! Get your bonnets, girls." She pulled on her own blue sunbonnet without stopping to tie the strings. The girls said they did not need sunbonnets.

"You get on the other side of the tomato vines, Tish," she commanded, "and, Jane, the bean patch. Slow, now, and quiet, not to scare the hens. And don't step on the plants more than you can help."

Jane had not known how excitable, how noisy, how stupid chickens could be. No sooner was the flock headed in the direction of the chicken pen than a rooster would suddenly lift himself high off the ground, fan his wings like a general rallying for a last desperate assault, and dash madly about-face towards the bean patch, with all the hens in headlong, flapping, squawking flight behind him.

"There's nothing in all creation that's got as little sense as chickens," Aunt Callie remarked when most of them had at last been shut within the pen. "Tish, you fetch another measure of feed from the bin and scatter it over the lot." It was too hot to chase the other hens. She advised the girls to cool off in the orchard creek. As for herself, there was Sunday dinner to be cooked.

Jane doubted whether Matron would approve of wading on Sunday, but Aunt Callie ought to know what was proper in the country. At the end of the pasture she and Tish stopped beside the hog-wallow to rest and watch the pigs. "They remind me of the time I fell off old Whitey into a mud hole," said Tish. "She's an obstinate old thing, that Whitey."

"How did you get the mud off?" Jane wanted to know.

"Aunt Callie," Tish replied tersely. "She poured water over me before she'd even let me into the kitchen. Uncle John said he thought at first I was one of the pigs that had learned manners and was coming to pay a call."

Jane laughed. "I'll put it in a story the first time the teacher tells us to write a composition. You'll appear in literature, Tish. Sammy Brown can draw the pictures."

Tish hitched up her overalls. "See that you make me beautiful—'fair as a lily.' Whatever you do, don't mention my freckles." Jane was the first over the orchard fence, but Tish was quicker with her shoes and stockings when they reached the creek. It was just right for wading, not too shallow and not too deep, with a sandy bottom and in some places stretches of slippery mud. When they had had enough of sun and water, they threw themselves down to rest in a shady place soft with tall grass.

"It's almost like being a gypsy," Jane remarked, stretching herself full length and looking up into the maze of green leaves overhead. She thought she might tell Tish about the gypsy princess and the brown gypsy baby. She had been wanting to tell somebody for ever so long. But Tish was not listening. She had found an ant on a mullein stalk and was trying to change its course with a grass blade.

Jane lay looking up into the tree. The crooked gray branches wound in and out like rivers among the green leaves. Only it was the rivers that stood still and the green leaf-country that moved. How far away the orphanage seemed, and how long ago the life she had lived there. Was it she who had played crack-the-whip with the boys behind the high fence, scuffing her shoes in the cinders?

She wished she would never have to go back—to be shut in behind the fence, with nobody belonging to her; to feel that other girls thought she was different from them because she lived in a Home and wore clothes that didn't fit.

She wondered if Matron would let her keep the white organdy dress. Even if she did, Jane was sure she wouldn't let her wear it. She'd think it wasn't sensible. Jane shook herself. "Don't be silly," she told herself. "Don't go spoiling your visit by thinking of what'll happen when it's over. You might as well not go on a visit if you're going to feel sorry because it can't last forever."

It was very still in the orchard. Tish was still poking at the ant. The birds were quiet, hiding from the hot August sun. Only the trees moved, as if the orchard were breathing, half asleep in sun and shade.

"We'll bring lunch next time," Tish planned. "You can't think what good lunches Aunt Callie packs—deviled eggs and ginger cookies and cucumber pickles and apple-butter sandwiches. But now we'd better go back for dinner. I'm hungry."

After dinner Molly joined the family in the shade of the horse-chestnut tree to look at the funny pages in the Sunday newspaper. She said Buster Brown and the Katzenjammers reminded her of certain others she could name.

"You're not referring to Jack and me?" Reuben tried to look hurt. "We've reformed." He gave her a teasing grin.

"Reformed?" Molly tapped him lightly on the head with the paper. "The day you two reform, storekeepers'll be giving their goods away and bankers will be inviting customers to help themselves to gold. No, the world's not coming to an end yet!" Her glance fell on Tish. "Been out without a bonnet again, I see," she commented. "The sunburn's so thick you wouldn't think you could see the freckles through it, but you can. They're beginning to pop out thick as measles."

"Oh, Molly, not honestly?" Tish wailed. She put her hand to the bridge of her nose as if she could feel the freckles.

"They're there, all right." Molly's voice was kinder. "No

use to fret; they'll fade out in time."

"But not before Martha Smith's party!" Tish's distress was real.

"Dab them with a mite of lemon juice and water before you go to bed, two or three nights running," Molly counseled. "That's my remedy."

Jane and Tish retired to the back porch and examined each other's faces carefully. Jane was sunburned bright pink shading in some places to red, but she had no freckles, Tish reported. Jane reluctantly had to admit that Molly was right. There were freckles all across Tish's nose, showing brownish pink through the sunburn. "They don't look bad, honestly," Jane tried to comfort her. But even when Jane assured her that the most popular girl in her favorite boarding-school story had freckles, "pale golden freckles scattered across the bridge of her tip-tilted nose," Tish was only slightly consoled. "My nose isn't tip-tilted." She spoke somewhat less dolefully, though she was far from being resigned. "It's just a plain snub nose."

"I think that's what *tip-tilted* means," said Jane. "When you call it that instead of *snub*, it's like saying a *simple* dress instead of a *plain* dress. It makes a difference, too."

Tish agreed that it did make a difference. Nevertheless, they would use the lemon juice. Without water. The juice would work better that way. Jane could have half the lemon; it would probably cure sunburn as well as freckles.

"We'll get up early tomorrow," Jane promised Aunt Callie. "I've never seen a threshing before, and I don't want to miss a minute. There are things I can do in the kitchen, too—peel potatoes and wash dishes and take the skins off tomatoes."

Aunt Callie thanked her and said she'd call on her for help if it proved necessary. Tish confided to Jane that she would much rather help in the field.

Next morning Jane volunteered to wash the breakfast dishes, and Tish dried them. Aunt Callie and Molly seemed to be made of rubber, they bounced back and forth so tirelessly from kitchen to springhouse, from springhouse to dining room, from dining room to kitchen. Jane was pleased to see inside the springhouse, where water from the spring—almost as cold as ice—flowed with a slow ripple over the top of a deep wooden trough and ran off in a tiny brook through an opening in the brick wall to join the pasture creek. A dozen watermelons, shining as if they had been polished, had lain all night on the damp springhouse floor to cool. Matron was always telling about the springhouse on her father's farm. Matron said it was much better than an icebox.

The threshing machine, drawn by four heavy-footed horses, turned into the lane. Uncle John sent Jack to tell them to enter the field from the highway; he didn't want the lane cut up. Light wagons began to arrive, and two or three buggies. Mrs.

Barry rode over with her husband to help with dinner. Grace would come later on horseback. Mrs. Barry did not look at all as Jane thought Grace's mother ought to look; she was fat and her hair was dark and there was a mole on her cheek. Grace must take after her father, Jane decided.

Jane and Tish shuttled back and forth like needles among magnets, now to the dining room to watch the table set, now to the kitchen; to the garden to help Molly gather ripe tomatoes and cucumbers and lettuce, to the corn patch to help bring in the roasting ears; and back to the kitchen, smelling of so many good things that it almost turned one's head. Other neighbors had joined Aunt Callie, all of them as busy as bees in a honeysuckle vine, except one. Mrs. Throttle leaned against the screen in the south window and watched.

"I'd like to be of some assistance, Miz' Scott," she was saying as Jane and Tish approached. "I'm not hardly able, my health's so poorly, but I says to my husband, I says, 'Josh, it's my bounden duty to help Miz' Scott with the thrashers.' An' he says, 'Ma, you hadn't ought to tucker yourself out, your health's so poorly.'"

Tish clapped her hand over her mouth to stifle a giggle, and motioned Jane to come outside. "That woman!" she whispered in Jane's ear. "Uncle John bet a whole dollar that she'd be here. She never misses a place where there's refreshments. Molly says she eats more than three healthy people. Aunt

Callie says it's not charitable to criticize her, but Molly thinks Aunt Callie is too soft-hearted for her own good." Tish tiptoed toward the kitchen. "Let's listen."

Molly spied them, however, and sent them to help Enoch carry water jugs to the field. He had to fire the boiler for the threshing machine, and they could drive the buggy back to the barn. Molly had sweetened some of the water with molasses, and put lemon juice in the rest, to quench the men's thirst and keep them from drinking too much when they were hot. Some preferred it one way, some another. The gray jugs held the molasses water.

Enoch scarcely exaggerated when he said it was hot enough in the field to fry an egg. The sun blazed down from a cloudless blue sky, and the earth, brown and parched under the short yellow stubble, sent up heat in shimmering waves. "You kin feel the hot plumb through the soles of your shoes," he said, "an' wrappin' round your ankles." And indeed they could.

The girls could have remained indefinitely, watching the sheaves fed into the great maw of the machine, and the grain, like a river of gold, pouring from one funnel and straw and chaff, yellow as brass, from the other. Thick black smoke belched from the engine and spread in a low flat cloud over the growing haystack. Jane had always wanted to slide down a haystack.

"It's no fun." Tish disdained it. "The straw is sharp as needles almost, and it goes through your clothes and scratches like anything." Jane thought to herself she'd like to try it anyhow. She would not mind a few scratches.

Uncle John sent the girls to the house; it was too hot in the field. When they said it wasn't, honestly, he laughed and said well, then, it was too hot for Whitey; she'd have a heat stroke. Before they reached the house they could smell the chicken frying. They were glad they had not stayed longer.

Aunt Callie let them pull the bell rope that hung from the

top of the smokehouse, to call the men to dinner. Jane had never seen so much food, even when the orphanage was crowded. Cook would certainly enjoy this. She often told Jane that cooking under Matron's supervision was not what she called proper cooking. She was used to having plenty to do with, butter and cream and eggs and a free hand at the grocery store. She got good and tired of having to serve up the same things day after day. Sometimes she wished the good Lord had never made the first cabbage. Once when Cook was in a good humor she and Jane had planned what they would have if Matron gave them a free hand. The banquet that Jane now surveyed, however, far surpassed their imaginings.

She listed the different dishes on her fingers, the better to remember them to tell Cook. There was corn—roasting ears dripping with butter as the men held them over their plates to eat; fried corn, and corn in succotash. There were green beans and little kidney-shaped butter beans; stewed tomatoes and tomatoes sliced with cucumbers on curly lettuce leaves. Jelly, blue grape, pink crabapple and red currant; green cucumber pickles and piccalilli and red-brown chili-sauce.

Jane and Tish and Grace Barry and two ladies waited on the table. They passed the hot rolls and saw to it that the oval side-dishes were replenished with coleslaw. They helped circulate the bowls of chicken gravy, to be generously spooned out over mashed potatoes.

And the fried chicken! High-piled platters were emptied, and still more was brought in. Jane had never seen anybody eat so fast or so much as the threshers. Wouldn't Matron give them a talking-to about saving their digestions! They said there was a thunderstorm brewing, and they would have to race to finish the field before the storm broke. They would come back to the house for the melons later.

Jane and Tish sat with Aunt Callie and the ladies at a table laid on sawhorses on the porch. There had been moments in the dining room when Jane feared there might be nothing left, but she need not have worried. She noticed that Aunt Callie ate almost nothing. She hoped she had had something to eat in the kitchen.

Aunt Callie told the ladies not to bother with clearing up, but they insisted. Didn't she always stand by at their threshings till the last dish was washed? Only Mrs. Throttle did not return to the kitchen. She sat on the porch and fanned herself with a palm-leaf fan and talked through the screen door. If she overdid her strength, laws a-mussy, who would take care of poor Josh?

The men straggled up from the field. The last load had been put through the machine, they said, and in record time. It was none too soon either, for lightning was flashing over the river way and dark clouds, edged with brilliant white and gold where the sun struck through, were building in the west.

They sat on the grass under the trees and ate the melons. They refused plates. Jane was glad there would be no more dishes for Aunt Callie and Molly to wash.

Soon after supper Aunt Callie went to bed. Uncle John said he was afraid she was worn out, but she said no, she only wanted her beauty sleep. Jack and Reuben lay on the grass and Uncle John relaxed in a chair which he dragged off the porch. He said he wished the rain had not passed them up; the corn fields needed a good soaking, the stalks were beginning to fire. Jack grumbled that the rain would hold off till the day he took Grace to the county fair.

Tish had been so quiet that Jane thought she was asleep, but at the mention of the county fair she bounced up. "Uncle John," she wheedled, "you'll take Jane and me to the fair, won't you?"

Before he could answer, the side door opened. In the half light, Jane saw Molly standing on the porch. She was looking down the lane as if she expected somebody, and at the foot of the lane stood a single-seated buggy, with the top folded back.

Molly crossed the porch. Jane noticed that she was wearing a hat and had on a dark skirt and light shirtwaist. She carried a small satchel. Without so much as glancing in their direction Molly walked in front of them across the yard to the lane. She walked as if she were a queen, with unhurried steps and her head held high.

At the entrance to the lane a man stepped out of the shadow. He took the satchel and said something in a voice too low for Jane to distinguish the words. Together the two walked down the lane to the waiting buggy.

In the little group under the tree nobody spoke until the buggy had passed from sight. Then Reuben gave a long whistle. "Now she's done it," he said. "I suspected it all along."

"Done what, Reuben?" Tish wanted to know.

"Eloped."

"Eloped? Really *eloped?*" Tish's voice expressed the same breathless awe that Jane herself felt.

Jack took up the conversation. "They're going to get married at the preacher's house and leave the horse in his barn. They're going to Chicago for a honeymoon. They'll be gone three days."

"Where did you find out so much?" Uncle John leaned forward to inquire. "She didn't tell you, did she?"

"No, Bill Healey did. Tom was obliged to tell Bill when he bought the railroad tickets. He asked Bill to flag the through train for them."

"Bill Healey had no business telling," Uncle John commented gravely. "He has a loose tongue."

"What did they elope for?" This from Tish. She was excited. "Did her father forbid her to get married?"

"They had their own reasons for eloping, no doubt," said Uncle John. "It's not our business to meddle. Molly's a good girl. She put it off until after the threshing was done. Not all girls of nineteen would have waited to help with the threshing. She's a worker, Molly is. She'll make Tom Anderson a good wife."

They sat in silence. A breeze sprang up from the south and set the leaves to whispering among themselves. A cicada shrilled close by, and far across the fields a dog bayed at the rising moon. The sky began to brighten in the east and as Jane watched, the harvest moon swung round and full and ruddy gold above the horizon.

Uncle John rose from his chair. "Bedtime, children," he said. "Bedtime for all four of you." His voice sounded tired. "It has been a long day."

11

THE SUMMONS

What's the matter with your nose, Tish?" Aunt Callie looked up from the eggs she was poaching for the girls' breakfast. "Do you feel all right?"

Tish nodded a forlorn yes and turned away.

"You look as if something's the matter with you," Aunt Callie pursued the subject. "You haven't got into a patch of poison ivy along the road, have you? And Jane too!" Jane blushed fiery red. "You're not sick, are you?"

"No'm." Jane's reply was too meek to be convincing.

"Come here to the window so I can get a good look at you both," Aunt Callie ordered. She took first one girl's chin and turned her face toward the sunlight, and then the other. "It doesn't look like measles," she noted thoughtfully, "and I don't know where you'd catch measles anyhow. Do you feel feverish, either one of you?" She laid a cool hand on their foreheads and felt their pulses.

"We're all right. Maybe we didn't sleep well." Tish sounded cross. "There's nothing the matter, honestly."

"Not sleep well? I never knew you not to sleep, Letitia Scott. Open your mouth—wide—so I can see if your throat's red." Aunt Callie's concern was mounting. "Maybe it's something you ate. I was afraid no good would come of that second slice of watermelon last night. You'd better both have a good dose of castor oil to be on the safe side." She searched among the bottles on the clock shelf.

Jane tried not to giggle, for she knew Tish was in no humor to think it funny; but the giggle slipped out.

Aunt Callie swung around, castor oil bottle in hand. She glanced sharply from one to the other. "You've been up to something," she said accusingly.

"Shall we tell?" Jane looked to Tish for permission. After all, it was Tish who was responsible, and Tish's nose was more blistered and fiery than her own.

Tish nodded. The nod managed to convey at the same time misery, shame, and struggling good humor.

"Lemon juice," Jane explained succinctly.

"Whatever are you talking about?" Aunt Callie was completely baffled. "It's not lemon juice at all; it's castor oil."

At that, both girls broke out laughing. She looked so bewildered, grasping the black-labeled bottle like a threat of calamity, that they quite forgot their burning, painful noses and thought only how funny she looked. The more they laughed, the more mystified she grew.

"I don't know what's got into you," she said, her kind face in troubled creases. "I declare, if you were feverish I'd think you were both out of your heads."

Tish collapsed on a kitchen chair, tears of laughter rolling down her cheeks. Jane leaned against the wall, trying to stop laughing long enough to muster breath to speak. "We put lemon juice on our sunburn," she managed finally. "The skin came off."

Aunt Callie's face was a study. She had been so distressed and worried that for a moment she could not grasp the humor of the situation. Then she too began to laugh. Uncle John stuck his head in to inquire what the joke was, but she motioned him away. Aunt Callie was discreet and kind. She had been a girl herself once; she knew that girls do not mind being teased about certain things, but certain things they do mind. "This is a private joke," she told him. "It's for the womenfolks of the family."

She set them bowls of sliced peaches and cream, and went to get the ointment the doctor had given her for a burned hand. The soothing lotion not only made their faces feel better; they looked better, as the girls observed with relief when they studied their noses in the kitchen mirror a few minutes later.

While they cleared the kitchen table and washed their breakfast bowls and plates so that Aunt Callie could start making peach butter as soon as she finished tidying up the other part of the house, Jane found herself feeling better and better. She began to hum a stave of *My Heart's in the Highlands.*

"What're you so happy about?" Tish queried morosely. She was almost certain the freckles were going to show in spite of the lemon juice.

"You can't think how nice it is not to be in the Home." Jane flipped a piece of soap high into the air with one hand and caught it deftly with the other.

Tish forgot her crossness long enough to be curious about what the children did at the Home. "You wouldn't like it," Jane told her. "You'd have to get up at half-past six and make your bed and tidy your washstand drawer and sweep under your bed and dust. After breakfast you help wash dishes or sweep or take care of babies or pull weeds or go on errands. Errands are best."

"Ugh, I'd hate it!" Tish made a face. "Do you ever have fun?"

"Of course. We play on the playground. Sometimes Matron lets us play quiet games indoors." Jane tried to make the Home sound lively, but her heart was not in her words.

"What if you don't want to work?" To Tish, for whom

work had a limited appeal, life in an orphanage sounded extremely tiresome and dull.

"You'd be in hot water with Matron. She can't abide a shirker."

"I'd run off," declared Tish. "Why don't you, Jane?"

"I've thought about it sometimes," Jane didn't mind admitting, "but I haven't any money."

"You could come to my house. We'd be glad to keep you till you earned some."

"It would cost a lot of money for a railroad ticket to get there." Jane appreciated Tish's offer but she wished her to understand the difficulties. "Anyhow, I don't have a really good reason to run away. Sometimes when I lose my temper and get mad I think I'll do it. But I most probably won't. They'd find me and bring me back. Boys try it, but they almost always catch them. And it's lots easier for boys to run off than girls."

Tish conceded that things were often easier for boys than girls. "Besides," Jane continued, as much to convince herself as Tish, "I'm lucky to have a nice place to live in like the James Ballard Memorial." Observing Tish shake her head and open her mouth to disagree, she added hastily, "Of course it wouldn't do for you, Tish. You're used to having a family of your own. I don't intend to stay in the Home always, myself. When I'm grown up I'm going to live in a house like other people."

Then, because she didn't want Tish to feel sorry for her, Jane boasted a little. She told about how she had had her fortune told by the gypsy princess, free of charge. She showed Tish the lucky star at the base of her forefinger.

Tish was impressed. "A princess!" She drew a deep breath. 'Oh, Jane, nothing exciting like that's ever happened to me." She was almost envious.

"Maybe she wasn't really a princess," said Jane. "Only I thought she looked like one."

"Of course she was," Tish maintained stoutly. "I'll bet she's the gypsy king's youngest daughter. They're always the most beautiful."

The two girls examined the palms of Tish's hands minutely, hoping to find a star of luck for her. But although some of the fingers had little clusters of lines at the base, they did not ray out like Jane's star. "Oh, Jane, you *are* lucky," Tish averred solemnly. "I always knew you were."

After midday dinner Jane and Tish washed the dishes, since the new hired girl had not yet come. The last clean pan had just been set in the pantry when Uncle John brought a letter for Jane. Even before she opened it, it seemed to her she knew what it said.

"I hope it isn't bad news." Uncle John stood looking at her, concern in his eyes. Aunt Callie was looking at her too, and

Tish, the damp dishtowel dangling from her hand.

Jane swallowed. "It's from Matron. Miss Fink has hurt her arm. I'm needed to help with the babies."

"You can't go! I won't let you!" Tish flung the dishtowel

violently at the table. "Uncle John, you won't let her, will you?" She was on the verge of tears.

"Must you go, Janie? Couldn't one of the others help?" Aunt Callie asked, smoothing her apron with short, anxious strokes. "If I wrote to Matron Jones, mightn't she let you stay out your visit?"

Jane struggled with temptation. Inside herself, she knew

she ought to go, but she rebelled. Let Matron get somebody else. Why should Jane be the one to give up her visit? It wasn't fair. But the inner self held firm. Jane shook her head. "No'm, I think I'd better go. Matron says Miss Fink's arm is in a sling. I'm to come right away."

"It's not fair! She said you could stay a month and now she won't let you! And we're having so much fun and there are loads of things we haven't done yet and I'll be left here all by myself." Tish was incoherent, between tears and anger. "I simply loathe and despise that Matron."

Seeing Tish so upset made it easier for Jane to get the upper hand over her own feelings. It eased the sharp hurt to know how much Tish cared. "Matron can't help it," she defended her. "I expect she's sorry. She wouldn't send if she didn't need me."

Tish stamped her foot. "I wouldn't stand it! Don't you stand it, Jane. Don't let her boss you. Run away, Jane. You can go to my house. Uncle John'll give you money, won't you, Uncle John?" She buried her tear-streaked face against his sleeve.

He stroked her curly topknot. "There, there," he attempted to soothe her. "I feel just as bad as you do, Tishie. But we mustn't interfere; we must let Jane do what she thinks is right. We mustn't make it harder for her."

"Next year Matron Jones will let her stay all summer,"

Aunt Callie promised, trying to cheer them all.

Jane felt grateful to Uncle John and Aunt Callie for making things easier. She was even more grateful to Tish, however. To see Tish lose her temper and cry did Jane almost as much good as if she had done it herself. It made her able to see things more plainly. When she thought about it, she was sure Matron had not spoiled her visit on purpose. She would not be unfair if she could help it. Things just happened like that sometimes.

"How soon must you go?" Uncle John inquired.

"On the first train I can, Matron says. They need me." Her voice had regained its steadiness.

"That's tomorrow morning," said Uncle John. "Tomorrow at eleven."

12

AT THE ORPHANAGE

WHEN Jane had been back at the Home a few days it was almost as if she had never gone away. Everything was as she had left it a few weeks earlier—the bare rooms, the cinder-covered playground, the high board fence. There was one difference, however; little Peter was not there.

At first she was afraid to inquire. There was still no infirmary, she remembered with a sudden sharp ache in her mind. Perhaps he had got sick and died. Maybe it was all her fault.

She had promised to do her best about an infirmary, but she had not even hinted to Mrs. Thurman to give one. She had even told her not to worry, they would get along without one. It hadn't seemed right to make Mrs. Thurman worry, because anybody could see that she needed new things herself. And Mrs. Thurman had to buy the house where the family moved in with chickens and a goat, although she said she couldn't afford it.

Then Jane thought of Peter, the dimple in his cheek, the way his fat little fingers closed around hers when she took him for a walk across the playground to the apple tree. If he was dead, maybe it was her fault. If there had been an infirmary for him to be sick in, he might have got well. She kept thinking about it after she went to bed; she couldn't go to sleep. She tried to pray; but not even God, she thought, could do anything about it if Peter was already dead.

At the risk of a scolding if Matron should catch her, she tiptoed downstairs to Miss Fink's room. A narrow band of light shone under the door. Miss Fink was still awake. Jane knocked softly, and Miss Fink, clad in a long brown wrapper that buttoned up to her chin, opened the door. "My goodness, child," she greeted Jane, "are you sick? Your eyes look as big as two burned holes in a blanket."

"No'm, I'm not sick. I wanted to ask about—about Peter. Did he die?"

"Die?" Miss Fink squinted her little dark eyes at Jane. "Die?" she repeated. "Why, not that I know of. Have you heard bad news about him?"

"I haven't heard anything. Nobody mentioned him."

Miss Fink's face cleared. She relaxed her clutch of the calico wrapper and let the hem sweep the carpet. She turned the gas light higher, the better to see her visitor. "Peter's adopted."

She was peering up at the gas mantle to see why it flickered. "I 'sposed you knew."

Jane's relief was so great that it was almost painful. Her mind felt like a tooth that goes on aching even after it has been pulled.

"Here, have a chair." Miss Fink drew up a carpet-covered rocking chair. "As long as you're already up, you might as well talk a spell. Matron's asleep. I heard her snore when I passed her door to get a pinch of soda from the kitchen."

Jane slid down into the chair, pulling up her knees and drawing the coarse nightgown down over her bare legs and feet. "Who took him?" she inquired, clasping her arms around her knees.

"I don't know their name. They was from some other state; Kentucky, it might be, or Indiana. They looked like nice folks; talked nice too. Matron says they've got a big farm—raise blooded stock." Miss Fink pulled her chair close so they could talk without raising their voices. "Matron was awful close-mouthed, but I overheard part. Peter's to take the place of their boy that died. They don't want that Peter should ever know he's not their'n. They want that he should forget the orphanage."

A wave of loneliness swept over Jane, chilling and disheartening her. Peter would forget about her. As long as she lived she would remember him, but he would never think of her. She felt cut off from other people, people who lived in houses and laughed and teased and joked and called each other loving names. For five weeks she had lived like one of them, as if she really belonged. Now she was shut away behind a fence. She would never get free again.

Miss Fink fumbled in her workbasket to find her crocheting. Jane blinked hard at the white buttons on the brown calico wrapper. "Don't be a stick-in-the-mud, Jane Douglas," she told herself resolutely. "Of course you'll get out of the orphanage. Don't you remember, you're going to earn money and go to college? And afterwards of course you'll live in a real house."

"I want you to know, Jane," Miss Fink was saying, "how bad I felt when Matron sent for you. Think of me spoilin' your visit! I did my best to prevent her, but she wouldn't listen. My foot slipped on the stair, an' I sprained my arm. It's them new bifocals the eye-doctor gave me. An' I was makin' some crochet to trim a dress to surprise you." She held up the lace for Jane to see.

"Oh, Miss Fink, it's ever so pretty! You shouldn't spend money for thread after that nice red pocketbook and two nickels."

Miss Fink was pleased that Jane liked the lace. "And now," changing the subject, "tell about the visits. There's no chance to talk when Matron's about."

It was a comfort to have Miss Fink listen with such interest. Jane described the white tub on four claws, and the parlor with the red satin curtains on top of lace ones. She told Miss Fink how old-fashioned most of Mrs. Thurman's things were, and that the house was old. Did Miss Fink think Jane ought to bother Mrs. Thurman about the infirmary?

Indeed, quite the contrary! Miss Fink believed it would be wrong to expect Mrs. Thurman to part with her money under the circumstances. The positiveness of Miss Fink's opinion freed Jane's mind of a heavy burden.

Jane told about the threshing and the ice-cream sociable. "Miz' Scott is sure a fine cake-maker," Miss Fink praised her highly. "I never et better than that piece of cocoanut you saved from your lunch. She must set a lavish table." She was particularly interested in the elopement. Jane could see that she was disappointed because there was so little to tell.

Sammy Brown returned a day or two later from a farm in the next county. The farmer and his wife had been called

away, and there was no one with whom to leave Sammy. Jane was glad to have his company, although they seldom had time to talk, since she was usually busy and Matron promptly set him to work in the vegetable garden.

One evening after supper as he and Jane sat on the front steps, he talked about the farm. He had worked hard, but the farmer and his wife were kind and he liked them. "I'm going to make a change," he told Jane. "Maybe not right away, but I'm going to make one."

She knew him so well that she could ask him what kind of change he meant. "Promise you won't tell?" The question was a matter of form. He knew she could be trusted to keep a secret. "Maybe I'll get adopted." He spoke in a low voice though nobody was near to hear. "Mind you, I said maybe."

"Oh, Sammy!" There was longing in her voice.

"I ain't supposed to know," he confided, "but Mr. and Mrs. Sawyer—they're the folks I was stayin' with—they talked one night after I'd gone to bed. They thought I was asleep but I wasn't, 'specially after I heard 'em mention my name. Mr. Sawyer was all for adopting me right off, but she held back a little. It wasn't that she didn't want me, you understand," he said defensively. "It's on account of this person that's sick. Because if she stays sick and has to come to live with 'em, they'd have to put her in my room. An' then where'd I sleep? Their house ain't very big. This person, this aunt I guess she is, well, from what I heard 'em say, she's awful cross. She doesn't like noise or children. If it wasn't for that, they'd take me quicker'n a wink."

"Maybe she'll go somewhere else to live," Jane suggested hopefully. She could see his heart was set on being adopted.

"They want to adopt me, all right." Sammy was not boastful; he was reporting what he had overheard. It bolstered his self-respect to repeat it, and helped strengthen his will to endure disappointment if disappointment should come. "Mr.

Sawyer said I was cut out to be a farmer, I was so handy; and his wife said I was handy about the house too, helpin' sweep and wash dishes. I tried awful hard, Jane. I kept hoping and hoping they'd ask me to stay on. The Sawyers is different from other folks I've worked for. Things like her making gingerbread special for me, and him takin' me to town every time he went."

Jane waited. She could tell from the way his hands were clenched that he was all wound up. "If they don't take me—" he muttered.

"You wouldn't, Sammy, you wouldn't?" Jane questioned anxiously.

He was defiant. "Yes, I would, Jane Douglas. If they don't take me I'll run off as sure as I'm sittin' here. I've had enough of being bossed by old lady Jones."

"Sammy, you wouldn't go now, with winter coming on before long?" she pleaded with him. "Why not wait, Sammy, till its springtime and you could sleep outdoors if you had to? Maybe you could earn money this winter and have a nest-egg saved up to buy a railroad ticket so you wouldn't have to walk all the way. It gets bitter cold in winter, Sammy, and you with nobody to take you in."

His eyes met hers. They were brown eyes, and even while she was so troubled for him she noticed that his eyes and the freckles thick on his nose matched in color.

"Maybe I'll wait." In spite of himself he welcomed an excuse for postponement. He yielded reluctantly, however. He must not let a girl think she was making up his mind for him.

Jane knew Sammy. She knew how he felt. "What we must do now," she was cheerfully matter-of-fact, as if the outcome were assured, "is to plan how you can earn money."

"I can earn." Sammy was on firm ground now. "Mr. Bates said he'd give me a dollar a week any time to help out in the grocery store after school."

"The only trouble is, Matron mightn't let you keep the money." Jane wrinkled her brows in thought.

Sammy's eyes lost their shine, his shoulders slumped. Then he braced himself and set his jaw. "I can get around that." He had a stubborn streak, and Jane could hear it coming out in his voice. "I'll tell old lady Jones I'm not earning but fifty cents, and keep the rest."

"That wouldn't be honest, Sammy."

"Well, then"—he hit upon what seemed to him a happy solution—"I'll tell her I'm earning fifty cents. That'll be the truth, because if I'm earning a dollar I'm sure earning fifty cents."

Jane did not quite like the solution. It still did not seem honest, though if you looked at the words, what they said was true. She made no further objection. Perhaps later they could think of a better way. She would not worry him now. "We must think of a place to keep your nest-egg," she said.

"Yes, if anybody saw it, they'd be sure to blab." There was no privacy in the dormitories. Everybody saw everything.

"If you ask Miss Fink to keep it, she'd never tell." Jane was not certain he would accept the suggestion, though she felt it was a good one. "She's helped me out of trouble many a time."

Sammy considered for a few moments before he replied. "If you're willing to stand for her, Jane, I guess I am. She's not so bad, old mousey Fink."

"And maybe," Jane reminded him hopefully, "maybe the cross old aunt will go somewhere else and you won't have to run away."

For a time they sat without saying anything. The sky was turning apple green where the sun had set, and tiny clouds drifted like feathers of gold toward the darkening horizon.

"Sammy," Jane asked, "do you remember your mother?"

"A little bit." He looked straight ahead at the board fence, but he was not seeing it. "Her eyes were blue, I think. She used to sing and laugh. I don't remember the words, but she used to try to get me to sing a song with her."

"What was your father like?"

"I never saw him to remember. He died when I was little."

Jane wished she could remember her father or mother. Sometimes she thought about them and wondered about them. Matron said it was written in the records that they came from Scotland and that they both died of typhoid fever when Jane was eight months old. Jane did not mention them to Sammy; she did not know whether he would be interested.

Later, when she knocked at Matron's door to return the dollar, Matron regarded it with surprise. She ran her fingers over the bill to find the pinpricks where the safety pin had gone through. "You didn't spend any of it?"

"No, ma'am. Twice I thought I'd have to break into it, but I didn't."

"Didn't you spend anything while you were gone?"

"Yes, ma'am, I spent two nickels. I bought Mr. Scott and Tish—she's their niece—an ice-cream soda apiece while we waited for the train to come. Mr. Scott bought me one."

"Where'd the two nickels come from?" There was a thin edge of suspicion in the words.

"Miss Fink gave them to me."

"Sit down," said Matron, settling herself comfortably in her big rocking chair. "Tell me about Mrs. Thurman. You think there's not much hope in that direction for an infirmary?" She did not seem particularly surprised or upset, Jane noted with relief.

"No, ma'am. Richie Matthews says her house is one of the oldest in town. It's not on the street where the rich people live, either. I noticed she didn't wear much jewelry, like Mrs.

Meadows." Jane still felt uncomfortable at the thought of India Maud's mother. "She's the banker's wife."

"Too bad the banker's wife's not on the Board," Matron commented dryly. "The James Ballard Memorial could do with a few rich ones." She dismissed the subject of the infirmary. "I was right sorry to break up your visit, Jane. If I'd known it was just a sprain Miss Fink had, I might have let you stay. But I guess you'd already had enough visit," she concluded briskly. It would not do to let Jane feel sorry for herself.

Matron was in a good mood. Jane decided to seize the opportunity to ask a favor. There might not be as good a chance again for a long time. She placed her feet squarely on the floor and sat erect. Matron did not approve of slouching. She cleared her throat. "Please, Matron, do you think you could let me earn money outside? A Baptist lady asked me if I would mind her baby sometimes for her. She said she'd pay me. Maybe there are other ladies who'd like to have me help out."

Matron looked thoughtful. "I might," she conceded after a suitable interval. "You're a sensible girl, Jane. You wouldn't squander the money like some."

"Oh, no, ma'am," Jane agreed eagerly. "I want to save it for—" She checked herself just in time. She had almost said for college. Matron would not approve of college; she would call it "highfalutin folderol." "For an education," Jane finished primly.

"A laudable ambition," Matron acknowledged, "very laudable. You might even go part way through high school. Miss Chapman says you're good at books."

Jane felt so triumphant at being allowed to earn money that she had to warn herself not to get puffed up; pride goes before a fall. But she understood now what Uncle John meant. Tish had said crossly that she didn't think Jane's lucky star was any good; it didn't keep the visit from being spoiled. Uncle John said that stars may be all right, but you make your own luck. And now Jane was making her own luck. She was going to earn money and go to college like Tish.

She must get permission for Sammy Brown, too. He bungled when he asked things for himself. Matron did not get on so well with boys as girls. Boys resented being ordered about and they often showed it. "Rebellious and ungrateful," Matron called them when they were stubborn. The girls were more docile, or at least succeeded better in concealing their resentment. They might sulk, but they rarely "talked back."

"I was speaking to Sammy Brown yesterday," Jane continued. She tried not to sound too eager or too determined. "He'd like to earn money too. He's a saving kind of boy. I don't believe he'd squander his money."

"What's he want to do?"

"Mr. Bates offered to let him work in the grocery after

school."

"M-mm." Jane held her breath until she saw the puckers begin to smooth out of Matron's lips. "I might let him." She grudged a little giving permission to Sammy. "He's steady; I guess 'twon't turn his head. He'll have to save his earnings, though; I'll permit no wasteful spending."

Day followed hot August day, each very like the others. Miss Fink no longer carried her arm in a sling and Jane had to do less of the heavy lifting of babies in and out of the cribs. She was not so tired now when she climbed upstairs to bed in the dormitory. Sometimes she and Miss Fink crocheted. Miss Fink said it certainly was kind of Mrs. Thurman to give all that nice lavender yarn for the shawl. Good yarn cost dear, and this was fine and soft enough for a baby's sacque.

Jane wore the yellow chambray dress to Sunday School. Miss Fink was voluble in praise of the Irish crochet, and even Matron remarked that Mrs. Thurman must have "re-fined" taste. It was too bad she was not rich enough to help the James Ballard more.

There was a substitute teacher for Jane's class, a Mrs. Sneed. She was a small fussy woman with tightly crimped hair of bright henna color. (Miss Fink sometimes touched up her hair with henna, Jane knew.) When Mrs. Sneed talked, her face broke into a network of fine wrinkles under the thick layer of white powder. She wore a breast pin of blue glass and dangling blue ear-drops. When the lesson was ended, she detained Jane to examine the lace on her collar and cuffs. She said she could copy any crochet pattern, she didn't need directions. All she needed was a close-up look. She picked and pulled at the lace, separating the stitches to count them.

Suddenly she let go of the collar and subjected Jane to a prying scrutiny. "Don't you live at the Orphanage?" Mrs. Sneed pronounced the word with a capital letter.

"Yes, ma'am." Without exactly knowing why, Jane felt embarrassed.

Mrs. Sneed sniffed. "I thought so, with that short cut of hair." She drew herself up to her tallest, which indeed was not very tall. "And you stand there and tell me that a girl living in a Charitable Institution" (more capital letters) "dresses in fine chambray and Irish lace!"

"No, ma'am." Jane's cheeks were burning, her eyes felt hot in their sockets, her breath came quick and short. She wanted to strike Mrs. Sneed, to hurt her; but she held on to herself. "No, ma'am," she had to say each word very carefully to keep from screaming it. "The orphanage didn't have anything to do with this dress. A lady in another town gave it to me."

Mrs. Sneed drew up the skin on her powdered nose, the way a cat does when it hisses. Even in the midst of her burning anger and humiliation the similarity struck Jane. Involuntarily she giggled. Brief though the little ripple of laughter was, it eased Jane's wounded pride of the bitterness of its sting.

Mrs. Sneed was taken so unaware, she was so completely at a loss to account for the smile that flickered across Jane's face, that she could only gasp. Gathering herself together with an explosive exclamation, she turned to flounce out of the pew in high dudgeon. Unfortunately for her intentions, however, the hem of her skirt caught on a nail. Her majestic withdrawal was abruptly terminated, like a raring horse suddenly reined short. "Oh, my silk petticoat!" she gasped, "my new silk petticoat!"

Jane stooped to free the caught skirt. "It's only a little snag, ma'am," she said politely. "It won't show much when it's mended."

Mrs. Sneed mumbled something about being much obliged. Under the white powder her face was purplish red. Her exit from the pew was marked by the same uneasy manner that characterized Aunt Callie's old red bantam hen when she had caught her tail in the gate and pulled out all the feathers.

Jane and Sammy walked back to the orphanage together after Sunday School. When she told him about Mrs. Sneed, how she had almost pulled the lace to pieces to find how it was made, and what she had said about living on charity, Sammy growled and clenched his fist.

"She's an old high-stepper," he said angrily, "a spiteful

old high-stepper." Neither was quite sure what 'high-stepper' meant, but it gave them solid satisfaction. Mr. Sawyer had applied the term to a lady store clerk who had offended him, and it seemed to fit Mrs. Sneed as if it had been made for her.

Jane was a good mimic, and her lively imitation of Mrs. Sneed's fall from toplofty pride at the sound of the snagging petticoat kept Sammy laughing to the very gate. It put Jane in a gay mood too, and gave her an unaccustomed appetite for boiled beef and boiled potatoes and cabbage.

After she had gone to bed she could not help thinking about Mrs. Sneed. It was strange that people held it against you because you lived in an orphanage. You couldn't help it any more than India Maud could help having a mother who was cross and complaining, or than Molly could help having a shiftless father. Of course you ought not to pay attention to what mean people said about you. Do your best and let your conscience be your guide, she told herself. Think about nice people, like the Scotts and Mrs. Thurman.

She wondered what Tish was doing now, and India Maud. India Maud's father sometimes let her stay up until he went to bed. Maybe this very minute she was thinking about Jane. They were a little bit alike, India Maud and Tish. They both had curly hair, they both liked to have good times, and they were both used to having their own way.

Jane wished she could be her own boss, not always doing

what Matron told her to do. Maybe she had a stubborn streak, like Sammy Brown. Now that she thought of it, she must have. Hadn't she insisted that Matron let her go to Cherry Valley? Hadn't she refused to let Cissie Matthews spoil her party? Hadn't she made the girls play the pirate game? And hadn't everybody had a good time!

She was glad she had a stubborn streak. If she did not have it she would be always getting discouraged, always ready to give up before she had half tried. But she must remember not to be contrary. There was a difference between contrariness and stubbornness. If you were contrary, you spoiled other people's good times.

"You're a lucky girl, Jane Douglas," she told herself. It made her almost solemn to think how lucky. "You've had two visits, and you've lived in two real houses. You've got a best friend. Not many girls have as nice a person as India Maud for best friend. You've a stubborn streak in you, and you were born with a star of luck."

☙ ☙ ☙ 13 ☙ ☙ ☙

JANE'S CHOICE

Blue Monday," Cook called it. Everybody disliked wash-day, but Cook most of all. On washdays she often threatened to throw up her job and get herself a better one. The smell of suds, she insisted, seeped into the cooking and made the beans and dried apples taste like soap.

"Nonsense, that's just another of your silly notions!" Matron entered the kitchen without warning. Although she spoke reprovingly, the reproof was without the tartness which customarily flavored it. She looked almost jovial as she barged skillfully between washtubs on one hand and the hot coal stove on the other, her stiff starched skirts swishing. "Oh, there you are, Jane. I wish to see you in my room. Leave the potatoes for Cook to peel. She has plenty of time and nothing else to do."

Cook scowled and muttered something under her breath.

She took good care, however, to keep the muttering so low that Matron could not hear.

"Yes, ma'am." Jane laid down the paring knife and dried her hands hastily on a corner of the kitchen towel. What could Matron want? It was clear that she did not intend to give her a talking-to. Matron was pleased about something. Pleased and excited. Jane began to feel excited too.

She waited until Matron had settled herself comfortably in the hollow of the wide rocking chair before she took a prim seat on the edge of the Morris chair. Matron did not like you to make yourself too much at home in her room; she said it showed a lack of proper respect. Matron surveyed her as if she knew a secret which she could not quite make up her mind to share. She folded her plump hands, and then unfolded the two forefingers and tapped them together several times. Something in the quick, nervous movement of the restless forefingers communicated itself to Jane—a sense of suspense, of momentous events pending.

"I've had two letters this morning." Matron gestured toward her darning basket where the letters lay in plain sight on top of a stack of black stockings, a square envelope of pale gray and a long white one. Matron made no move to reach for them; she must remember what they said. "They concern you. They're from Mrs. Scott and Mrs. Thurman."

Jane's heart leaped, her thoughts quickened with nameless

hope. She pressed down hard first with one foot and then the other, to ease an almost overmastering impulse to seize the letters and read for herself what they said. Why must Matron be so everlastingly slow? Why must she keep twiddling and fiddling with her fingers?

Matron cleared her throat like a preacher about to begin a sermon. "They both say you behaved well. Mrs. Scott says you were helpful about the house and well brought up, and Mrs. Thurman says I deserve great credit."

Jane's heart sank. She didn't know what she had expected from the letters, her hope had been too breathless, too swift to take definite shape, but she had expected something more than this.

"As I always tell you children, Jane"—Matron launched into one of her familiar sermons—"bring up a child in the way he should go and he'll behave properly when he's out of your sight. As the twig is bent, I believe it firmly, and I always do my conscientious best to see that it's bent in the right direction. Remember that, Jane, when you're far away from the James Ballard Memorial and I'm not by to advise you."

A vague implication in Matron's phrasing, a suppressed excitement that tinged the familiar words with unfamiliar promise, stirred Jane's hopes again. She gripped the edge of the Morris chair to hold herself still. What was Matron lead-

ing up to? Was there something else written in the letters, something important that she was keeping secret?

Matron leaned forward in the rocking chair to rest an impressive hand on Jane's knee. "Jane, Mrs. Scott says in her letter that she and her husband would like to adopt you and give you a good home and education, as if you were their own daughter."

Matron waited for the words to sink in, but they did not sink, they swirled and sang and echoed around Jane's head. She felt so light and empty that it seemed to be only the weight of Matron's hand that held her in her chair, to prevent her from floating upward to circle and swirl with the echoes against the ceiling.

Matron dropped the other hand upon Jane's knee. "And likewise Mrs. Thurman too."

Jane's thoughts danced round and round in such a dazed whirl that she hardly knew whether the sounds she heard were echoing inside her mind or outside it. "Oh, Matron." She drew a long, incredulous breath. "Oh, Matron Jones!"

Matron's faded blue eyes met hers, steadying and reassuring her. "It's the gospel truth," she said; and unwilling to let slip an opportunity to point a moral, "It comes of behaving properly, like a good girl."

"Oh, Matron!" It was as though every word that Jane had ever known had been forgotten except those two and she must keep repeating them over and over. "Oh, Matron!"

"You can take your choice between the two places. There now, don't get so excited you lose your common sense. Take your time to think it over, like a sensible child. I'll leave you alone while I go see to the washerwoman so she doesn't put too much bluing in the sheets, like last week." Matron looked back for a moment from the doorway as if she might volunteer a helpful hint about the most sensible choice for Jane to make, but she contented herself with repeating, "Take your time, take your time. Don't make up your mind too hasty."

Deep, deep down in some far quiet corner of her heart Jane knew that she had already made her choice, but she forced herself to shut the door of her attention against that choice and consider what she ought to do. She almost wished Mrs. Scott and Mrs. Thurman hadn't both asked her, she wanted so much to be in both places and it would be so hard to give up either one. If only she were two persons and could live in both houses at once! Or if she could stay part of the time in one and part in the other! It made her feel bad to think she couldn't have them both, when they wanted her and she wanted them.

"But you can't," she reminded herself sensibly before she had time to feel too sorry about it. "Being adopted means having a family of your own, like other people. Who ever heard of having two families at once?"

She must decide which family she most wanted to belong to for ever and ever. It was like choosing a best friend, the way she and India Maud had chosen each other. She must use common sense, she mustn't be hasty, she must bend the twig right, as Matron warned her.

Never in her whole life had she had so many good times as during that week on the farm with Uncle John and Aunt Callie. They had not acted as though they felt sorry for her or thought she was different from them because she had to live in a Home. They treated her like a person who belonged, exactly the way they treated Tish. Uncle John teased her and jollied her and Aunt Callie was nicer and kinder than any aunt in a library book. And Tish was just like a real cousin— better than the very nicest one in *Eight Cousins*.

Without even closing her eyes she could see the rambling white house, dappled with sunshine and shade; the dark leaves of the horse-chestnut tree curving under the wind, the golden-stubbled fields where the wheat had been threshed, and the green orchard breathing soft and slow. She smelled the fresh scent of new-cut hay, and Aunt Callie's biscuits hot from the oven.

If she went to live with Aunt Callie and Uncle John they would send her to college with Tish, and they could have midnight feasts and get into scrapes and have fun together. She wanted to go to college. She wanted to learn ever so many things. She wanted to read hundreds and hundreds of books, hard books like the ones Jack and Reuben kept on their shelves.

If she lived with Mrs. Thurman maybe she could not go to college. Mrs. Thurman might not be able to afford it. It would be common sense to choose Aunt Callie and Uncle John so she would be sure of going to college.

Mrs. Thurman had been kind too, but for some reason that Jane had not been able to figure out no matter how much she thought about it, she sometimes felt clumsy and tongue-tied when she was with her. Mrs. Thurman seemed somehow to be different from other ladies Jane had been acquainted with. It wasn't only because her voice was quiet and she wore such pretty soft-colored dresses, even early in the morning; it wasn't because she carried her head high. Molly carried her head high too, but Jane never felt dumb with Molly.

Dumb didn't exactly describe how she felt, either; there was something about Mrs. Thurman that kept pulling Jane toward her. It was like a note of music, deep and quiet, that found its way to Jane's heart and made an answering music there. Except that the music seemed to stay bottled up tight inside her, and she didn't know how to let Mrs. Thurman know it was there.

Maybe it was because Mrs. Thurman seemed lonesome and Jane wanted so much to be of help and didn't know how, that she felt the way she did. She longed to do a favor for Mrs.

Thurman to show how she felt, but Mrs. Thurman did not need favors. She had everything she really needed.

Jane drew a sharp breath. She put her hands on her knees to steady them, she suddenly felt so excited again. What if Mrs. Thurman needed her to be company for her? Aggie couldn't be much company because she had Abner, and she almost always stayed in the back part of the house.

To her surprise she felt a lump swelling in her throat. She was so happy that she felt almost like crying. From the very first moment that she had seen Mrs. Thurman sitting by the window in the back parlor she had longed to stay with her, to grow up to be just like her. If she had the whole wide world to choose from, she'd always, always choose Mrs. Thurman.

Common sense spoke up to remind her of college. It would not be sensible to give up going to college just because she'd rather live with Mrs. Thurman than with Aunt Callie and Uncle John. Her inner self refused to be shaken by any arguments that common sense could raise. "Do your best and let your conscience be your guide. It's right to choose the person that needs you most," she asserted boldly. Uncle John and Aunt Callie had each other and two big boys besides; they would never be lonesome. Mrs. Thurman had nobody.

"Well, Jane," Matron bustled in, "have you had time to make up your mind?"

"Yes, ma'am," answered Jane. "I choose Mrs. Thurman."

Matron's round, pinkish face broke into a shiny smile, her blue eyes beamed, her head nodded in vigorous approval. Jane was relieved. She had been half afraid Matron might think she was not being sensible. "A laudable decision I call it, very laudable. And if I may say so, most convenient for me too," she remarked somewhat mysteriously.

She jerked open the table drawer and drew out a sheet of paper. "You must write a letter to thank Mr. and Mrs. Scott for their kind offer."

"Oh, and to say I love them." In all her life Jane had never spoken out loud about loving anybody, but now the word sounded right and natural.

Matron did not notice. She had still an important secret to tell. "You probably wondered what I meant, Jane, when I said it was very convenient for me that you picked on Mrs. Thurman. I didn't tell you before, Jane, because I didn't want to influence you in any least way. I wanted you to make your own choice, fair and free."

Matron lifted a hand dramatically, as if she were about to pronounce a benediction. "Jane, would you ever believe it? She's going to give us money to build an addition for an infirmary! She says she's sending an architect next week. You're the first I've told; not even Miss Fink knows. I couldn't believe my own eyes when I saw it in the letter. I had to read it three times over and it still seems too providential to be true."

Though Jane smiled and nodded to show she was pleased about the infirmary, she hardly heard what Matron was saying. Later on she would have time to think about it and be glad, but just now she could think only about her own shining, singing happiness.

"Wake up, you old stick-in-the-mud." She could hardly keep from shouting the words out loud for the whole world to hear. "Wake up! Do you know what's happened to you?" The words soared and sang like the music of a brass band and church bells ringing, like a choir of angels with golden harps and trumpets. "You're adopted, Jane Douglas; you're adopted!"